BREAKING THE ICE

LADY HEARTSWELL

CENTURIA BOOKS LLC

CONTENTS

CHAPTER ONE

THE BULLET AND THE BYLINE

The silence in the apartment isn't peaceful; it's thick, like settled dust. I straighten the throw pillows for the third time, aligning the corners until they are geometrically perfect. This is the routine. This is the sanctuary I spent ten years building, brick by boring brick.

But my pulse is a traitor. It hammers against my ribs, a trapped bird throwing itself against the cage.

God, I want to scream. I want to open the window and let the freezing rain ruin the hardwood floors. I starve for a mistake, for a jagged edge, for something that proves I'm actually alive and not just preserving myself like a specimen in a jar.

Yet, when the floorboards creak, I freeze. When the wind howls, I check the deadbolt. That's the rot at the center of me—this paralyzing terror of the very chaos I crave. I am desperate to burn, to feel the heat of a real life, but I am so terrified of the ash. So, I sit. I smooth the fabric of the couch. I wait for the silence to swallow me whole, praying that today, something—anything—will finally break me open.

The phone vibrating on the coffee table sounds like a gunshot.

"Gage," I answer. My voice is steady. The woman who just wanted to scream is gone, replaced by the instrument of the state.

"We have a hit on the Salazar safehouse. Ten miles south of the San Ysidro crossing," Miller says. His voice is tight. "Local PD is scared to touch it. It's quiet. Too quiet."

"I'm en route."

I grab my keys, my badge, and the Sig Sauer P320 waiting in the lockbox. The apartment door shuts behind me, sealing the silence inside. I don't look back.

*

The air in the stash house tastes like copper and bleach.

It's a standard sprawling stucco nightmare in the hills of Tijuana, hidden behind a high privacy wall and bougainvillea that looks too bright against the peeling paint. I move through the fatal funnel of the front door, weapon raised, every nerve ending stripped raw.

Silence hangs heavy here, too. But this isn't the suffocating quiet of my living room. This is the silence of a graveyard.

Three bodies in the entryway. Cartel foot soldiers. The shots were professional. Two to the chest, one to the head. No wasted brass. The blood is tacky, turning black on the saltillo tile. Whoever did this didn't come for drugs. They came to send a message.

"Clear," I whisper to myself, sweeping the kitchen. More bodies. A half-eaten plate of tacos sits on the counter next to a severed hand.

I step over a dead sicario, his chest cavity ruined by a shotgun blast. My boots stick to the floor. The DHS windbreaker feels like a target on my back. I'm alone. Miller is ten minutes out with the federales, but I couldn't wait. Protocol dictates I hold the perimeter. Protocol hasn't saved a single victim in six months.

A sound cuts through the death.

A whimper. Low, wet, and desperate.

It's coming from the back utility room. I stack up on the door-frame, checking my corners. If there's a shooter left, this is where they'd be. The ambush point.

I kick the door. It swings inward, hitting the wall with a hollow thud. I pivot, sweeping the room with the muzzle of the Sig.

Empty of humans.

But in the corner, chained to a exposed water pipe, is a creature that barely resembles a dog. It's a pit bull, grey and white, skin stretched so tight over its ribs it looks like a skeleton wrapped in parchment. One ear is torn, fresh blood dripping onto the dirty concrete. It cowers as I enter, pressing itself into the filth, shaking so hard its teeth click together.

The chain is heavy, industrial grade, wrapped around a neck chafed raw. There's a bowl just out of reach. Bone dry.

Rage, hot and sudden, flares in my gut. I can handle the dead narcos in the hallway. I can handle the corruption, the politics, the wasted years. But this? Cruelty for the sake of cruelty?

"Hey," I say, my voice softening. I lower the weapon. "It's okay."

The dog flinches. It expects a boot. It expects pain.

I holster the Sig. Bureau policy screams in my head—*never un-holster in an unsecured zone.* I ignore it. I kneel on the grime-coated floor, making myself small. I pull a protein bar from my tactical vest, tear the wrapper with my teeth, and break off a piece.

"I'm not going to hurt you." I hold out the food.

The dog stretches its neck, nose twitching. The desperation wins out over the fear. It takes the food, lips gentle against my fingers.

"Good boy." I reach for the heavy clasp on the collar. It's rusted shut. "I'm getting you out of here."

I struggle with the mechanism, the metal biting into my thumbs. I'm so focused on the lock, so focused on this one small thing I can actually save, that I miss the shift in air pressure behind me.

I don't hear a footstep. I don't hear a breath. I just feel the sudden, crushing weight of another presence in the room.

My hand drops to my holster.

"Don't."

The voice is low, deep, and scraped over gravel. It commands obedience not through volume, but through absolute certainty.

I freeze. Slowly, I turn my head.

A man stands in the doorway. He fills the frame, blocking out the light from the hallway. He isn't cartel. Cartel is flash, gold chains, and loud shirts. This man is a shadow cut from the night.

He wears a suit that costs more than my annual salary—charcoal grey, Italian cut, fitting him with a precision that borders on architectural. It's ruined, though. Splatters of dark blood stain the pristine white cuff of his shirt and the lapel of the jacket. He doesn't seem to care.

He holds a suppressed Beretta at his side, his finger resting casually along the trigger guard. He isn't pointing it at me. He doesn't need to. The threat radiates off him like heat from a furnace.

My eyes travel up. He's tall, over six-two, with a build that suggests violence isn't just a trade, but a religion. Broad shoulders taper to a trim waist. His face is a ruin of handsome features—sharp cheekbones, a strong jaw darkened by stubble, and a scar that slices through his left eyebrow, vanishing into hairline.

But it's the eyes that stop my heart. Dark, intelligent, and devoid of anything resembling mercy.

He steps into the room. I tense, ready to draw, ready to die in this laundry room if I have to.

He ignores me completely.

He holsters his weapon in a shoulder rig beneath his jacket, the movement fluid, practiced. He walks past me, lowering himself to one knee beside the dog. The expensive fabric of his trousers meets the filth of the floor.

The dog, which had been trembling at my touch, suddenly goes still. It sniffs the man's hand. The man's knuckles are bruised, split open from fresh violence.

"Ciao, bello," the man murmurs. The harshness of his voice evaporates, replaced by a low, rumbling warmth. He runs a massive hand over the dog's head, careful of the torn ear. "They didn't feed you, did they? *Bastardi.*"

He reaches into his jacket pocket and pulls out a precise folding knife. With a flick of his wrist, the blade locks. I flinch, hand tightening on my grip.

He doesn't look at me. He slides the blade between the dog's neck and the rusted collar. With a single, controlled twist, the leather snaps. The chain falls away.

The dog leans into him, letting out a long, heavy exhale. The man scratches behind the dog's ears, his expression softening into something that looks painfully human. For three seconds, he is gentle. For three seconds, the monster in the suit is kind.

Then he stands up.

The change is instantaneous. The warmth vanishes. The humanity snaps shut behind steel doors. He turns to me, and the temperature in the room drops twenty degrees.

He looks me over, starting at my boots and ending at my eyes. It's not a sexual appraisal; it's a tactical dissection. He is weighing my worth and finding it lacking.

And God help me, my body betrays me.

Even covered in blood, even radiating a lethal aura, the man is a masterpiece of masculine aggression. The suit jacket strains across a chest thick with muscle. His hands, now hanging loose at his sides, are large, veined, capable of snapping a neck as easily as he cut that collar. There is a kinetic power to him, a vibrating potential energy that makes the air feel thin. He is danger personified, and my traitorous brain floods with adrenaline and something darker, heavier. I want to know what those hands feel like when they aren't being gentle. I want to know if that rigid control ever breaks.

"You flagged the fatal funnel when you entered," he says. His voice is ice now. "Your footsteps are heavy. You breathe too loud."

My jaw tightens. "Federal Agent. Hands where I can see them."

He doesn't move his hands. He tilts his head, a dark amusement lighting his face. "If I wanted you dead, Agent, you wouldn't have heard me come in. You would have bled out on the floor thinking about your pension."

"Who are you?" I demand, standing up. I keep my hand near my weapon, though I know, with sickening certainty, that he's faster than me.

"Someone doing your job," he says. He glances at the dog, then back to me. "The Cartel left this house an hour ago. You're late. The government usually is. Always chasing ghosts, always burying the bodies after the fact."

"I have backup en route," I lie. "Heavily armed."

"You have two federales who are on Salazar's payroll and a partner who handles paperwork better than a pistol," he counters smoothly.

He knows. How does he know? "Take the dog. Leave the premises. This place is going to burn in five minutes."

"I'm not going anywhere. You're a suspect in a multiple homicide."

He steps closer. The scent of him hits me—sandalwood, gunpowder, and the metallic tang of blood. He invades my personal space, towering over me, forcing me to tilt my head back to maintain eye contact. I refuse to step back. I refuse to show him the fear coiling in my stomach.

"I am not a suspect," he says softly, his voice dropping an octave. "I am the consequence. And you, *tesoro*, are out of your depth. Go back to your desk. Go back to your reports. The world has teeth, and you are soft."

"I'm not soft," I snap.

He looks at my hand, hovering near my gun. Then he looks at the dog, now free and nudging my leg.

"You stopped for a dog in a kill zone," he says. "That is soft. It is also the only reason you are still breathing."

He turns his back on me. The dismissal is total. It stings worse than a slap.

"Wait!" I shout.

He pauses at the door. "Five minutes, Agent Gage. If you are here when the accelerant catches, not even your badge will protect you from the heat."

He disappears into the dark hallway.

I stand there, heart slamming against my ribs, the taste of copper in my mouth. My name. He knew my name.

I look down at the dog. It looks up at me with large, trusting eyes.

"Come on," I whisper, grabbing the scruff of its neck. "Let's go."

We run. We clear the front door just as the first whoosh of ignited gasoline sucks the oxygen out of the house. The windows blow out, showering the driveway in glass.

I drag the dog to my SUV, shoving him into the back seat. The heat from the fire beats against my face, hot and furious. I watch the flames crawl up the stucco walls, devouring the evidence, devouring the bodies.

A black sedan idles down the hill, watching the fire. As I look, the tinted window rolls up, and the car slips away into the night, a shark disappearing into black water.

Dario Ferri.

I know the face now. I know the scars. The Capo of the West Coast. The ghost the agency has been trying to pin down for three years.

He called me soft.

My hands grip the steering wheel until my knuckles turn white. The fear is gone, burned away by the fire and the insult. In its place is a cold, hard resolve.

I am not soft. I am the Shield. And if he thinks he can burn down my city and walk away, he is going to learn that the Shield can be used to bludgeon, too.

I start the engine. The dog puts its head on my shoulder, letting out a long sigh.

"Yeah," I tell him, watching the fire reflect in the rearview mirror. "I hate him too."

*

The drive back to San Diego is a blur of red taillights and rain. I drop the dog—I'll call him Buster, for now—at the shelter run by my sister-in-law. She promises to keep him off the books. I promise to pay the vet bills.

My phone rings again. It's Miller.

"Merritt, where are you? The Federales arrived, place is an inferno. Did you engage?"

"Negative," I say, my voice flat. "House was torched when I got there. No visuals on the perps."

I lie effortlessly. I'm not giving Dario Ferri to the locals. He's mine.

"Get back to the office," Miller says. "Something's happened. It's bad."

The ominous tone in his voice makes the hair on my arms stand up. "What is it?"

"Just get here. The Director is in the war room."

I hang up. The wipers slash across the windshield, fighting a losing battle against the storm. The city lights of San Diego blur into streaks of neon.

I park in the underground structure, the concrete cold and damp. The elevator ride up to the 14th floor feels like an ascent to the gallows. The bullpen is usually buzzing with low-level noise—phones ringing, keyboards clacking, agents trading war stories.

Tonight, it is silent.

Heads turn as I walk in. People I've worked with for ten years look away. They study their shoes. They study their screens. No one meets my eyes.

A cold stone forms in my stomach.

I walk straight to Miller's desk. He's sitting with his head in his hands. He looks up, his face grey.

"What?" I demand. "Did we lose the warrant for the port seizure?"

Miller stands up slowly. He looks like he's aged ten years since this morning.

"Merritt," he says, and his voice cracks. He reaches for a file on his desk. It's a crime scene photo, face down.

"Tell me," I say, the command sharp.

"It's Jack," he whispers.

My partner. Jack Reynolds. The man who taught me how to clear a room. The man who bought me a beer every time my cases hit a wall. He was supposed to be on leave. He was supposed to be at his kid's soccer game.

"Jack?" I stare at him. "What about him?"

Miller slides the photo across the desk. He flips it over.

The world stops. The fluorescent lights hum, a buzzing insect sound that drills into my skull.

It's Jack. He's tied to a chair in what looks like a warehouse. His badge is shoved into his mouth. His chest...

I squeeze my eyes shut, but the image is burned into my retina. The brutality is medieval. It's a message.

"Where?" I choke out.

"Found him an hour ago. warehouse district. Gang unit thinks it was MS-13 initiation," Miller says, but the words sound hollow. "Standard hit."

"Standard?" I slam my hand on the desk, the sound cracking like a whip. "Look at the knots, Miller! Look at the precision! That isn't a gang initiation. That's an execution."

I grab the file, flipping through the preliminary report. My hands are shaking. Not from fear this time. From a rage so pure it feels like holy fire.

"I want the drive," I say.

"Merritt, you're too close..."

"I want his hard drive, Miller! He was working something off the books. He told me last week he found a thread."

"Evidence locked it down," Miller says, stepping between me and the hallway. "Director explicitly ordered you to stand down. You're compromised."

"Compromised?" I laugh, a harsh, jagged sound. "I'm the only one who isn't blind."

I shove past him. I don't go to the evidence locker. I go to my desk. I log into the remote server Jack and I set up two years ago—a mirrored backup for when the red tape got too thick. A dead man's switch.

I type the password. *Buster.* The name of the dog he always wanted but his wife wouldn't let him get.

The screen flashes green. Access granted.

One folder. Uploaded three hours ago.

I open it. It's a map. A blurry satellite image of an island off the coast of Baja. *Isla de la Sangre.* Blood Island.

And a jagged list of IP addresses. Trafficking routes. Money laundering fronts.

I run the first IP address through the database. It bounces through three proxies in Singapore before hitting a server in San Diego.

A shell company. *Ferri Imports.*

The world tilts on its axis.

Dario Ferri.

He was at the stash house. He cleaned up the bodies. He told me I was chasing ghosts.

Did he kill Jack?

I think of the dog. I think of the gentle way he cut the collar. I think of the cold, dead eyes when he looked at me. *I am the consequence.*

If he killed Jack, I will burn his world down until there is nothing left but ash and bone.

But if he didn't... if he was at that stash house hunting the same people Jack was hunting...

I pull the thumb drive from the computer. I shove it into my pocket.

"Gage!" The Director's voice booms from his office doorway. "My office. Now."

I look at the Director. I look at the sea of agents who are too scared to look back. The system. The shield that is supposed to protect us. It didn't save Jack. It won't save the next one.

I turn my back on the Director. I walk to the elevator.

"Gage! If you walk out that door, you're done!"

I hit the button. The doors slide open. I step inside and press 'G'.

"I'm done," I say to the closing doors.

The metal slides shut, severing me from the only life I've known for fifteen years. I am free falling. I am terrified.

But for the first time in my life, I am not waiting for the silence. I am going to make some noise.

I will find Dario Ferri. And I will make him scream.

CHAPTER TWO

GHOSTS IN THE NEON

The weight of the Sig Sauer P320 against my hip bone is the only honest thing left in the world.

Everything else is a lie. The "protect and serve" decal peeling off the side of the cruisers. The condolences from the Director, delivered with the plastic sincerity of a politician looking for a soundbite. Even the rain smearing the windshield of my personal SUV feels fake, like Hollywood tears sprayed from a hose to set a mood.

Jack is dead.

The thought doesn't land like a blow. It settles like silt in my lungs, choking off the air slowly. I don't see his face when I blink. I see the report. I see the glossy 8x10s Miller tried to hide. The wire. The burns. The badge shoved into a mouth that used to tell terrible dad jokes about his kid's goalie skills.

They turned a good man into meat to send a message.

I downshift, the engine growling as I merge onto the 5 South, heading toward the Gaslamp Quarter. The city lights blur into streaks of radioactive color.

The agency wants to bury it. Gang violence. Random. Tragically unavoidable.

I touch the thumb drive in my pocket. The plastic is warm. Jack found the thread, and they killed him for it. That thread leads to an island that shouldn't exist, and an IP address that routes straight to the heart of the city's vice.

Ferri Imports.

Dario Ferri.

The name sits on my tongue like a curse. I should have put a bullet in him at the stash house. I had the angle. I had the justification. But I froze.

No. I didn't freeze. I *watched*.

The memory hits me harder than the whiskey I wanted to drink an hour ago. I see his hands—large, scarred, violent hands—cradling the pit bull's head. I see the way his thumb brushed the torn ear. For three seconds, the monster took the mask off, and there was something underneath that looked like pain.

That's why I didn't shoot. Because for a split second, in that blood-soaked laundry room, he felt more human than the badge I wear.

I grip the steering wheel until the leather groans. That hesitation got Jack killed. I let the wolf walk away, and now my partner is cold on a slab.

Never again.

The GPS pings. *The Obsidian.*

It's not a warehouse. It's a fortress of glass and black steel sitting on Prime real estate, masquerading as a nightclub. The line of hopefuls snakes around the block—girls in dresses that cost more than my car, guys with watches that could feed a village. They shiver in the rain, desperate to get close to the fire, unaware that the man tending it burns everything he touches.

I park in a loading zone three blocks away. I don't care about the ticket. I don't care about the badge in my pocket, either, except as a tool to breach the perimeter.

I check the Sig one last time. Chambered. Safety off.

I'm not here to arrest him. I'm here to look him in the eye and see if he flinches when I say Jack's name. And if he does—if I see even a flicker of guilt in those dead, dark eyes—I'm going to burn his kingdom down with him inside it.

*

The bass hits me before I even clear the velvet rope. It vibrates in my sternum, a deep, rhythmic thud that mimics a heartbeat.

The bouncer is a slab of beef with an earpiece and an attitude. He steps in my path, a wall of muscle and cheap cologne.

"Private event, sweetheart. List only."

I don't slow down. I don't speak. I flash the gold shield in my palm, holding it high enough for the strobes to catch the reflection, but low enough that he has to look down.

"Federal Agent," I say. My voice is unrecognizable. It's stripped of all the polite fiction I use at the office. It's jagged metal. "Move."

He hesitates. He sees the wet hair, the tactical boots, the eyes that haven't slept in thirty hours. He does the math.

He steps aside.

I push through the heavy double doors into the sensory assault. The air is thick, humid with sweat and expensive perfume. Red lasers slice through clouds of artificial fog. Bodies grind against bodies on the dance floor, a writhing mass of hedonism desperate to forget the morning.

I hate them. I hate their laughter. I hate their ignorance. They dance while good men die in the dark.

I scan the room, ignoring the flashes of skin and the spilling drinks. I dissect the space like a tactical grid. Exits. Blind spots. Security details.

The floor is chaos, but the mezzanine is control.

A glass balcony overlooks the pit. Shadows move up there, watching the cattle below.

I head for the stairs. A security guard at the bottom steps forward, hand raising to stop me. I don't break stride. I slam my shoulder into his chest, using my momentum to knock him off balance, and flash the badge directly in his face before he can recover.

"ICE," I lie. "We have a creditable bomb threat. You want to be the one explaining to Mr. Ferri why his club is swarming with bomb squad in ten minutes, or do you want to let me clear the VIP section quietly?"

Fear flickers in his eyes. Not fear of the bomb. Fear of the name *Ferri*.

He backs off. "Upstairs. Don't cause a scene."

"I am the scene," I mutter, taking the stairs two at a time.

The air gets colder as I ascend. The noise dampens, swallowed by soundproofing designed to keep the screams of the party separate from the business of the management.

The mezzanine is dimly lit, furnished with black leather booths and tables made of polished slate. It's quieter here. Deadlier. The men sitting at the tables aren't dancing. They're drinking scotch and discussing profit margins on human misery.

And there he is.

He sits in the center booth, the axis around which this whole dark world spins.

Dario Ferri.

He's discarded the ruined grey suit from the stash house. Now he wears black. A black dress shirt, unbuttoned at the collar, sleeves rolled up to reveal forearms corded with muscle and ink. A faint tattoo of a serpent winds around his left wrist, disappearing under the fabric.

He isn't drinking. He isn't talking. He's watching the dance floor below with the detached boredom of a god watching ants drown.

My stomach drops. Not fear. Recognition.

It's the stillness. Everyone else in this room is moving—gesturing, drinking, fidgeting. Dario is absolute zero. He occupies the space with a terrifying gravity.

I remember the heat of the fire at the stash house. I remember the smell of gasoline. And I remember the way he looked at me, dismissing me as *soft*.

Soft.

I reach into my jacket, fingers brushing the grip of my gun, but I pull my hand out empty. Not yet.

I walk toward him.

His security detail—two men who look like they chew glass for fun—start to rise.

Dario doesn't turn his head. He simply lifts one finger.

The guards freeze. They sit back down.

He knew. He knew I was here the moment I stepped onto the stairs. Maybe even before.

I stop at the edge of his table. My shadow falls over his glass of sparkling water.

"You're hard to kill, Agent Gage," he says.

His voice is exactly as I remember it—low, scraped over gravel, vibrating with a dark resonance that makes the hair on my arms stand up.

He slowly turns his head.

The impact of his gaze is physical. Those eyes. Black, intelligent, and utterly void of warmth. But there's something new there tonight. A spark. A curiosity. Like he's looking at a puzzle box he hasn't quite figured out how to open yet.

"I don't die easy," I say. My voice is steady, despite the adrenaline flooding my veins. "And I don't go away."

"Evidently." He gestures to the empty seat opposite him. "Sit. You look like you're about to collapse."

"I'd rather stand."

"Sit," he commands. It's not an offer. It's an order wrapped in velvet.

My knees ache. My head throbs. I sit. Not because he told me to, I tell myself, but because if I fall over, I can't shoot him.

"You cleaned the house," I say. "But you missed a spot."

I pull the thumb drive from my pocket. I slide it across the polished slate table. It stops inches from his hand.

He looks at it. He doesn't touch it.

"IP addresses," I say. "Routing back to this building. From a computer belonging to a dead federal agent."

The air between us changes. The ambient noise of the club fades away, leaving us in a bubble of high-pressure silence.

Dario's expression doesn't change, but the muscle in his jaw feathers.

"Dead?" he asks. The word is quiet.

"Don't insult me." I lean forward, invading his space. I want him to smell the rain on my clothes. I want him to see the bloodshot veins in my eyes. "Jack Reynolds. You knew him. You probably signed the order."

Dario picks up the drive. He turns it over in his long fingers. He handles it with the same terrifying dexterity he used with the knife on the dog's collar.

"I know the name," he admits. "He was... persistent. Like you."

"He was tortured, Ferri. They used a blowtorch."

My voice cracks on the last word. I hate myself for it. I hate the weakness.

Dario's eyes snap to mine. The boredom vanishes. For a second, the predator is fully alert.

"Here?" he asks. "In San Diego?"

"South of the border. Found him three hours ago."

Dario closes his hand over the drive. He leans back, the leather of the booth creaking. He looks toward the dance floor, his profile sharp against the flashing lights. He looks angry. Not the explosive anger of a man caught, but the cold, calculating fury of a man whose chessboard has been kicked over.

"I didn't kill your partner, Agent."

"Your tech says otherwise."

"My tech says someone used my servers to route traffic," he corrects. He looks back at me. "If I wanted your partner dead, he would have simply ceased to exist. No body. No torture. No message. I don't leave messy tableaus for the police to find. It's bad for business."

"You expect me to believe you?"

"I expect you to use that brain you're so proud of," he snaps. The sudden aggression makes me flinch, my hand twitching toward my hip.

He tracks the movement. His mouth curves, but it's not a smile. It's a warning.

"You think you're the hunter," he says softly. "But you walked into the lion's den with a service weapon and a grudge. You aren't hunting, Merritt. You're trespassing."

Merritt.

The way he says my name—familiar, possessive—sends a jolt of heat through my chest that has nothing to do with anger. It pisses me off.

"I have enough on this drive to bring a RICO case down on your head," I bluff. "I can bury you."

"You have nothing," he counters. "You have ghosts and echoes. And if you try to use that drive, the same people who killed your partner will kill you long before you reach a grand jury."

He tosses the drive back to me. It clatters on the stone.

"Take it. Go home. Feed the dog."

"His name is Buster," I say stupidly.

"A fits name for a survivor." He stands up.

The movement is fluid, unfolding his height until he towers over the table. The shift in power is immediate. Sitting, we were almost equals. Standing, he is a skyscraper, and I am the pavement.

"Where are you going?" I demand, standing up too fast. The room spins.

"To clean up a mess," he says. He buttons his jacket. "Someone is trying to start a war between my organization and your agency. They killed your partner to provoke you. And because you are emotional, and reactive, and *soft*, it worked."

"Stop calling me that." I step in his path.

It's a mistake.

He stops. He's six inches from me. I have to tilt my head back to look him in the eye. I can smell him—sandalwood, expensive tobacco, and the metallic tang of something dangerous.

He looks down at me. His gaze drops to my mouth, lingers for a heartbeat that feels like an hour, then snaps back to my eyes. The air between us is electric, charged with violence and a confused, terrible attraction that makes my knees weak.

"Prove me wrong," he whispers.

He steps around me.

"Ferri!" I grab his arm.

The muscle under the sleeve is hard as iron. He stops, looking at my hand on his arm like it's a curious insect. He doesn't shake me off. He just waits.

"If I find out you're lying," I say, my voice trembling with the effort to keep it level, "I won't arrest you. I will come back here and I will end you."

He leans in. His lips brush my ear. The sensation is scorching.

"If you find out I'm lying, *tesoro*, you won't have to coming looking for me. I'll be the last thing you see."

He pulls away. The warmth of his body vanishes, leaving me cold in the supercooled air of the club.

He signals his guards. They flank him, moving like a phalanx of shadows toward the private exit.

I stand there, clutching the thumb drive, my heart hammering a frantic rhythm against my ribs.

I should follow him. I should call it in.

But I don't.

I look at the drive. *Isla de la Sangre.*

He said someone is trying to start a war. He said he didn't do it.

My gut says he's telling the truth. My badge says he's a liar.

But my gut also remembers the way he touched the dog.

I shove the drive into my pocket. I turn and walk toward the stairs, my legs heavy.

Jack is dead. The system is compromised. And the only man who seems to know what's actually happening is the devil himself.

Fine.

If I have to dance with the devil to burn this island down, then I'll let him lead. But I'm wearing the lead shoes.

I push through the crowd, out into the rain. The cold water feels like a baptism.

I'm not soft.

I unlock my car, tossing the wet jacket into the passenger seat. I check the Sig again.

I'm not soft.

But as I stare at the neon sign of *The Obsidian* reflecting in the puddle, I realize the terrifying truth.

I wanted him to stay close. When he leaned in, when his breath hit my skin... I didn't want to pull my gun. I wanted to lean back.

I slam the car into gear.

The war has started. And I'm already losing ground.

Chapter Three

BALLISTICS AND BREATH

The rain outside *The Obsidian* hits the pavement like bullets. I stand by my car, keys digging into my palm, staring at the black reflective glass of the club.

I should leave. I should drive until the gas light comes on, file a report that will be redacted before the ink dries, and go home to an empty apartment. That is the safe play. That is the protocol.

But the engine block is cold, and the heat in my chest isn't anger anymore. It's instinct.

A gray van idles at the service entrance. No lights. No plates. The slide door is cracked open an inch. I know that posture. I know the stillness of men waiting for a green light.

Sicarios.

They aren't here for the music.

The realization hits my nervous system before my brain catches up. They are here for Dario. And if they take him out, I lose the only lead I have on Jack's murder. I lose the map to the island.

"Damn it."

I drop my keys. I draw the Sig.

I don't go through the front. I sprint for the service corridor, the wet asphalt slick under my boots. The van door flies open. Three men in tactical gear spill out, suppressed rifles raised. They are moving to breach the rear exit.

I don't shout a warning. I line up the sights on the lead man's vest and squeeze the trigger.

The shot cracks the night wide open. The lead man drops, screaming, clutching his thigh. The others spin, muzzles flashing. Brick dust explodes near my face, stinging my skin.

I dive behind a dumpster, heart slamming a frantic rhythm against my ribs. I wanted a war? I found one.

I pop up, fire two suppression shots, and scramble for the steel service door before they can pin me down. I kick it open and spill into the back hallway of the club.

The bass is muffled here, a low throb in the walls. I scramble up the service stairs, taking them three at a time. My lungs burn.

I burst onto the mezzanine level just as the glass wall at the front of the VIP section shatters.

The hit team from the van wasn't the only one. A second team rappelled from the skylights. The club floor below is a stampede of screaming civilians, but up here, it's a kill box.

Dario is still at his table.

He hasn't taken cover. He stands in the center of the chaos, a calm void in the storm. He holds a heavy, silver-plated pistol in one hand, firing with a rhythmic, terrifying precision. *Bang. Bang. Bang.*

Three attackers rush the stairs. His security detail is down—one dead, one bleeding out on the carpet.

"Ferri!" I scream, vaulting over a leather sofa.

He turns. For a fraction of a second, the muzzle of his gun tracks me. I see death in the black pits of his eyes.

Then he recognizes me. He doesn't lower the weapon; he pivots, firing past my ear.

A man behind me drops, a hole in his forehead.

"You came back," he roars over the gunfire.

"Get down!"

I tackle him. It's like hitting a marble statue. He doesn't stumble, but the momentum carries us both behind the heavy slate bar just as the wood paneling above us disintegrates under automatic fire.

We are pressed together in the dark, smelling of spilled scotch and gunpowder. The air is thick with dust.

"You have a terrible sense of timing, Agent," he growls.

"Shut up and reload."

I check my magazine. Six rounds. The enemy is closing in. I can hear their boots crunching on the glass.

Dario ejects his spent magazine. His movements are a blur of efficiency. He racks the slide.

"On three," he says. His voice is steady. No fear. Just calculation.

"One."

"Two."

"Three."

We rise together.

It is a dance of violence. I take the left; he takes the right. The Sig bucks in my hand. I double-tap a man in a balaclava coming over the railing. Dario moves with a predator's grace, his shots deliberate, heavy. He doesn't just kill; he erases threats.

We move down the corridor, back-to-back. I feel the heat of his body through his suit jacket, a solid wall of muscle protecting my spine. Every time I pivot, he counters. It's seamless. We aren't two strangers; we are two halves of the same weapon.

A gunman bursts from a private room on the left. My gun clicks empty.

I freeze.

Dario doesn't. He pistol-whips the man, the sound of metal on bone sickeningly loud, then kicks him over the railing to the floor below.

He grabs my vest, hauling me into the private office. He kicks the door shut and shoves a heavy oak desk in front of it.

Silence falls, heavy and ringing.

We are alone in the sudden quiet. The only light comes from the neon sign flashing outside the window, painting the room in strobes of red and black.

I lean against the wall, sliding down until my boots hit the floor. The adrenaline dump leaves my hands shaking. I fumble for a spare magazine, but my fingers are numb.

Dario stands in the center of the room. He checks his weapon, then holsters it. He looks at me.

And God help me, I look at him.

The violence has stripped away the polished veneer of the business-man. His hair is messy, falling over his forehead. The top three buttons of his shirt are gone, ripped open in the struggle.

I stare. I can't help it. His chest is heaving, the white fabric plastered to skin slick with sweat. Underneath, he is carved from granite—slabs of pectoral muscle, the deep groove of his sternum, the visible ridges of abdominals that look hard enough to break a hand on. His forearms are exposed, veins roping over heavy, dense muscle that shifts as he flexes his hands.

He is terrified aggression given form. He is a masterpiece of lethality. My mouth goes dry, a thirst spiking in my throat that has nothing to do with dehydration. I want to touch the ink winding around his wrist. I want to trace the map of scars on his knuckles with my tongue.

It is a primal, stupid urge. It is the biology of survival demanding I find the strongest thing in the room and cling to it.

"You're bleeding," he says.

His voice breaks the spell.

I touch my cheek. My fingers come away red. A graze from the brick dust. "I'm fine."

He crosses the room in two strides. He invades my space, towering over me, sucking the air out of the small office. He doesn't offer a hand to help me up. He reaches down, grabs me by the tactical vest, and hauls me to my feet.

He slams me against the wall.

My head cracks against the plaster. It hurts, but the pain is distant, dull compared to the electric shock of his body pressing into mine. He pins my wrists above my head with one hand. His grip is iron. I couldn't break it if I wanted to.

And I don't want to.

"Why did you come back?" he demands. His face is inches from mine. His eyes are wild, dilated, searching my soul for a lie.

"They were going to kill you," I gasp.

"So?"

"So I need you."

"Is that the only reason?"

His hips grind against mine. Hard. Unforgiving. There is no space between us for protocol, for badges, for laws. There is only the heat of the fight and the fact that we are both still breathing when we shouldn't be.

"Let me go," I whisper, but I don't struggle. I tip my head back, exposing my throat.

"No."

He lowers his head. He smells of violence and rain.

"You had a clear shot, Merritt. You could have let them finish it. You could have walked away clean."

"I don't walk away," I say.

"No," he murmurs, his gaze dropping to my mouth. "You run into the fire."

He crashes his mouth onto mine.

It isn't a kiss. It's a collision. It's a claim of territory. His lips are rough, demanding, punishing. He tastes of copper and expensive scotch. He kisses me like he fought in the hallway—with total, devastating control.

I make a sound in my throat, a desperate, broken noise, and kiss him back. I bite his lower lip. I taste his blood.

My hands are pinned, but my body arches into his. I need this friction. I need this pain to ground me. The world outside is dead partners and corruption and lies, but this... this heat, this weight, this man... this is real.

He releases my wrists. I should push him away. I should draw my knife. Instead, my hands tangle in his hair, pulling him closer, deepening the kiss until I can't breathe, until I see stars behind my eyelids.

His hand slides down my throat, over my chest, gripping my hip with enough force to bruise. He lifts me, pressing me harder against the wall. I wrap my legs around his waist, the friction of denim against wool clothes electric.

For a moment, we aren't enemies. We are two survivors trying to consume each other before the darkness breaks down the door.

He pulls back, gasping. His forehead rests against mine. His eyes are black fire.

"You are trouble, *tesoro*," he rasps. "You are going to get me killed."

"I just saved your life," I pant.

"You saved me for yourself." He runs a thumb over my swollen lip. The touch is startlingly gentle. "Now we are bound in blood."

The door rattles. Someone is trying to breach.

The moment shatters.

Dario drops me to my feet. The predator mask slides back into place. He draws his weapon.

"Can you shoot?" he asks, not looking at me.

I pick up my gun. I rack the slide on my last magazine. My hands are steady now.

"I don't miss twice," I say.

He glances at me. A corner of his mouth lifts—not a smile, but an acknowledgment. A salute from one monster to another.

"Good," he says. " Because we are leaving. My boat is at the marina. If you want the truth about the island, you're coming with me."

"And if I say no?"

"Then stay here and explain the bodies to the police."

He kicks the desk away from the door.

I look at his broad back. I can still taste him on my tongue. The burn of it scares me more than the gunmen in the hall.

I holster my weapon.

"Lead the way."

CHAPTER FOUR

BALLISTICS OF A LIE

The Jaguar tears through the slick streets of the Gaslamp Quarter, the engine a low, predatory growl that vibrates through the chassis. Rain lashes the windshield, blurring the neon lights of the city into streaks of radioactive color.

I don't look at her. If I look at her, I'll crash.

Merritt sits in the passenger seat, knees drawn up, turning the Sig Sauer over in her hands. She isn't trembling. Most people, even the ones who carry badges, shake after a firefight. The adrenaline dump leaves them hollowed out, their nervous systems misfiring.

Not her. She's vibrating, yes, but it's the hum of a machine running hot, not a structure about to collapse. She smells of cordite, expensive leather, and the unique, metallic scent of rain on hot pavement.

I grip the steering wheel. The leather groans under my hands. My knuckles are white. Not from the stress of the hit—I've survived worse on a Tuesday—but from the effort of not reaching across the console.

I want to touch her.

The urge is irrational. It's violent. It sits in the back of my throat like a swallowed stone. I want to wipe the smear of blood from her cheek. I want to feel the pulse hammering in her neck to make sure she's still alive. I want to drag her into the dark and keep her there, safe from the bullets and the politics and the rot that killed her partner.

"You're driving too fast," she says. Her voice is rough, damaged by the smoke and the screaming.

"I'm driving efficiently," I correct. "There's a difference."

"Where are we going?"

"My marina. It's secure."

"And then?"

"And then you go home, Agent Gage. You file your report. You lie to your superiors. And you forget you ever saw me."

She laughs. It's a sharp, jagged sound. "Forget the man who just helped me kill six cartel enforcers in a nightclub? That's going to be hard to omit from the paperwork."

"You'll manage. You're resourceful."

I glance at her then. I can't help it.

Her silhouette against the rain-streaked window is the only holy thing left in this godforsaken city. I've memorized the rhythm of her breathing, the precise hesitation before she clears the chamber of her weapon, the way the passing streetlights catch the stray threads of her coat. It's a hunger, sharp and violent, gnawing at me. I want to cross the distance. I want to grab her hand, pull her close, and drag her out of this mundane life before the storm hits. I want to be the one who saves her. I *need* to be the one.

But my boots are nailed to the floorboards.

If I step forward, I shatter the glass. If I answer this pull, I drag her into the blood and the mire with me. I crave her proximity like oxygen, yet the thought of her eyes widening in terror—terror caused by *me*, by the truth I carry—freezes my marrow. I am desperate to touch her, to finally prove she's real, but I'm terrified that I'm contagious. Safety is a lie, but it's a lie she still believes in. Who am I to break it? I'd rather watch her from the shadows and starve than step into the light and watch her burn.

She catches me looking. Her eyes are wide, dark pools reflecting the dashboard lights. There is no fear there. Just a challenge.

"You called me soft," she says quietly.

I look back at the road. "I did."

"I just put two rounds in a moving target at thirty yards. Am I still soft?"

"Marksmanship isn't hardness, Merritt. It's mechanics." I downshift, the car jerking as we hit the industrial sector near the docks. "Hardness is knowing the system you serve is the same beast feeding the thing you hunt. Hardness is walking away when you know you can't win."

"I don't walk away."

"I know." My voice drops. "That's why you're going to die."

I pull the Jaguar into the private garage at the edge of the marina. The steel gate rattles shut behind us, cutting off the world. The silence that follows is heavy, pressurized.

I kill the engine.

"Get out."

She bristles. She shoves the gun into her holster and exits the car, slamming the door hard enough to rock the suspension. I get out slowly, adjusting the cuffs of my ruined shirt. The pain in my shoulder is a dull throb—a graze, nothing more—but it anchors me.

She stands under the harsh fluorescent lights of the garage, looking like a battered angel of vengeance. Her hair is plastered to her skull. Her lip is swollen where she bit it during the kiss.

That kiss. It tastes like copper in my mouth.

"I need the intel," she says, extending a hand. "The thumb drive. And whatever else you have on the island."

"No."

She steps into my space. She has no survival instinct. "That drive is evidence in a federal murder investigation. Give it to me."

"If I give it to you, you'll take it to your Director. You'll ask for a warrant. You'll assemble a task force." I walk around the front of the car, forcing her to turn, to track me. "And by the time you get your rubber stamp, the island will be scrubbed clean. The girls will be moved. And you will be found in a ditch with your own badge in your mouth."

She flinches. It's microscopically small, a tightening of the muscles around her eyes, but I see it.

"My Director is a good man," she insists, though the conviction is thin.

"Your Director is a politician. And politicians are cheaper to buy than sicarios."

I stop in front of her. I loom. I use every inch of my height, every ounce of the violence I carry in my frame, to intimidate her. I want her to run. I want her to hate me. It's the only way she survives.

"Jack trusted him," she whispers.

"And Jack is dead."

I reach out. She tenses, hand twitching toward her hip, but she doesn't draw. I take her chin in my hand. Her skin is cold, wet from the rain. My thumb brushes the cut on her lip.

She sucks in a sharp breath. Her pupils dilate, swallowing the iris.

"You want to play the hero," I murmur, lowering my head until our foreheads almost touch. "You want the badge to mean something. But out here? In the dark? The badge is just a target."

"I'm not afraid of you, Dario."

"You should be." I slide my hand down her throat, resting it over her pulse. It hammers against my palm, a frantic bird trapped in a cage. "I am not the Shield, *tesoro*. I am the thing the Shield cracks against."

"Then break me," she challenges. Her voice is breathless, wrecked. "If you're so hard, break me."

The invitation hangs in the air, thick and intoxicating. My body responds instantly, blood rushing south, muscles coiling. I could take her here. Push her back against the hood of the car. finish what we started in the club. It would be rough. It would be exorcism.

But it would bind her to me. And I cannot do that to her. Not yet.

I drop my hand. I step back, putting three feet of cold concrete between us.

"Go home, Merritt."

The rejection hits her like a physical blow. She blinks, dazed, the heat in her eyes cooling to confusion, then hardening into ice.

"You're holding back evidence," she says, her voice flat. The agent is back. The woman is gone.

"I'm holding back a funeral." I turn my back on her, walking toward the keypad that opens the door to the docks. "I will handle the island. I will handle the cartel. You stay in your lane. Write your parking tickets. Chase your low-level dealers."

"You can't do this alone," she yells at my back. "They have an army!"

"I have leverage." I punch in the code. The lock buzzes. "And I don't have to follow the law."

I open the door. The smell of the ocean—salt and rot—floods the garage.

"Dario!"

I pause. I don't turn around.

"If you go to that island without me," she warns, "I will hunt you down. And I won't be coming to arrest you."

"Good," I say. "Bring plenty of ammo."

I step through the door and let it slam shut. The lock engages with a heavy, final thud.

I stand there in the dark of the walkway, listening. I hear her scream in frustration. I hear the dull *thump* of her boot kicking the Jaguar's tire. Then, silence.

I wait until I hear the service door open and close, until I hear her footsteps fade toward the street.

Only then do I let myself breathe. My hands act on their own, shaking out a cigarette from the silver case in my pocket. I light it, the flame illuminating the scars on my knuckles.

She's going to try the system. She has to. It's her religion.

And when the system fails her—when it spits her out and leaves her bleeding—she'll come back.

I walk down the dock toward the *Vesuvius*. The boat is black, sleek, a shadow on the water.

I need to prepare. The island isn't just a drug lab. Jack Reynolds found something else on that drive. Something that scared him enough to hide it.

I pull my phone from my pocket. I dial the only number that matters right now.

"It's me," I say when the line connects. "Clean the club. Pay off the police. And get the boat ready."

"We move tonight, Capo?"

"No," I say, flicking the cigarette into the dark water. "We wait."

"Wait for what?"

"For the Shield to break."

CHAPTER FIVE

THE BLOOD CONTRACT

M y apartment is a tactical failure.

I realize this the moment the lock on my front door disengages. I didn't turn the key. I'm standing five feet away, a bag of frozen peas pressed to my swollen lip, staring at the deadbolt as it slides back with a smooth, oiled *click*.

I reach for the Glock on the kitchen counter. My hand closes around the grip just as the door swings open.

Dario Ferri steps into my sanctuary like he owns the mortgage.

He fills the frame. The hallway light behind him casts his shadow long across my cheap laminate flooring. He's changed out of the ruined suit from the club. Now he wears a charcoal wool coat over a black turtleneck that emphasizes the dense, violent geometry of his upper body. He looks expensive. He looks calm. He looks like a shark swimming through a aquarium tank, indifferent to the glass.

I raise the Glock. "Get out."

He doesn't stop. He steps inside and closes the door behind him, engaging the lock with a dismissive flick of his wrist.

"Put the gun down, Merritt. If I wanted you dead, I would have used the fire escape."

"Give me one reason not to put a hole in your chest."

"Because you have terrible aim when you're concussed." He walks past me. He actually walks past the muzzle of a loaded federal weapon to inspect my living room. "And because I found the pilot."

My finger freezes on the trigger. "What pilot?"

"The one who flew your partner's body to Tijuana."

He turns to face me, hands in his coat pockets. The casual arrogance of it makes my teeth ache. This is my home. This is the one place where the filth of the job isn't supposed to touch me, and he's standing there critiquing my lack of furniture with his eyes.

I lower the gun, but I don't safe it. "Talk."

"Not here." He gestures to the window, where the streetlights of San Diego bleed through the blinds. "Your walls are thin. And I suspect your neighbors are the type to call the police if they hear the word 'cartel' spoken above a whisper."

"I am the police," I snap.

"You are a bureaucrat with a badge and a vendetta. There is a difference." He moves toward the kitchen, invading the space where I eat, where I exist. He picks up the file folder I tossed on the table earlier—Jack's autopsy report.

I lunge for it. "Don't touch that."

He catches my wrist.

The contact is electric, jarring. His hand is large, the skin rough with calluses that tell a story of violence inflicted by hand, not just by order. He doesn't squeeze. He just holds me there, a static force halting my momentum.

"He was cut apart while he was alive," Dario says. His voice is devoid of pity. It is a statement of fact, cold and heavy as a tombstone. "The cartel calls it *la limpieza*. The cleansing. They wanted him to scream out his secrets."

"I know what they did," I whisper, my throat tight.

"Do you?" He pulls me a fraction closer. The scent of him—gun oil, sandalwood, and the metallic tang of rain—floods my senses. "Do you know how long it takes a man to die when they start with the extremities? Do you know what he told them to make it stop?"

"Shut up."

"He told them nothing," Dario says softly.

The air leaves my lungs. I stop fighting his grip. I look up at him, searching the obsidian depths of his eyes for a lie. I find only a dark, terrible certainty.

"How do you know?"

"Because if he had talked, my operations in Baja would be ash right now. He protected the case. He protected *you*."

He releases my wrist. The loss of pressure leaves a phantom burn on my skin.

"The pilot gave up the coordinates," Dario continues, turning back to the table. He pulls a folded nautical chart from his coat and spreads it over the autopsy photos, covering the horror with logistics. "It's not just a stash house. It's a fortress. *Isla de la Sangre*. Blood Island."

I look at the map. A red circle marks a jagged speck of land off the coast of Ensenada. It's in international waters, just barely.

"I need a boat," I say, tracing the coastline. "I can requisition a cutter, but it'll take forty-eight hours to clear the red tape."

"You don't have forty-eight hours. The storm front coming in from the Pacific hits tomorrow night. They'll move the girls before the swell gets too high."

"How do you know about the girls?"

He looks at me. The mask of the businessman slips, revealing something ancient and weary beneath. "Because that is what this faction does. They don't just move product, Merritt. They break things. People. Children."

A muscle feathers in his jaw. It's the first sign of genuine emotion I've seen since the dog.

"My boat is fueled," he says. "My team is dead or in the hospital. I can get us to the island. I can navigate the reefs in the dark. But I can't move the assets once we're on the ground."

"Assets?"

"The victims. I'm a criminal, Agent. If I show up with a boatload of traumatized children, the Mexican Navy sinks me. If you show up... you are the United States Government."

The realization slots into place like a magazine in a well.

"You need my badge," I say.

"I need your cover." He leans his hands on the table, looming over the map. "I provide the transport and the firepower. You provide the legitimacy. We burn the place to the ground, we get the girls out, and you call in the cavalry to clean up the mess."

"And you?"

"I disappear into the smoke."

"That's illegal. It's aiding and abetting a known felon."

"It's justice," he corrects. "Or is your book of rules more important than the cages on that island?"

I look at the map. I look at the gun on the counter. Then I look at him.

He is a monster. I know this. I've read his file. I've seen the crime scene photos of men who crossed him. He is rigid structure, cold violence, and unyielding code. He is a predator who dominates the physical space with a terrifying grace.

But he is also the only man willing to walk into hell with me.

The system didn't save Jack. The Director told me to stand down. The law is a shield that has rusted through, and I am tired of hiding behind it.

"We do it my way," I say. "No executions. If they surrender, they live."

Dario straightens. A dark amusement touches his mouth, gone as quickly as it appeared. "If they surrender, Agent Gage, I will buy you a pony. These men do not surrender."

"I mean it, Ferri."

He steps around the table. The space in the kitchen evaporates. He backs me against the counter, his hips boxing me in. It's an intimidation tactic, a test of will.

"You want to give orders?" he murmurs, his voice dropping to a gravel-rough register that vibrates in my sternum.

"I am the federal agent. This is my operation."

"This is a war zone. And in a war zone, you do not command what you cannot kill."

He places a hand on the counter on either side of my waist. I am trapped. I should knee him in the groin. I should draw my knife. But I don't. My heart hammers a traitorous rhythm against my ribs—not fear, but a spike of adrenaline that tastes like iron.

He leans down. His face is inches from mine. I can see the pores of his skin, the faint white scar cutting through his left eyebrow. He assesses me not as a woman, but as a weapon he is deciding whether to holster or discard.

"You are proficient, Merritt. You shoot straight. You have courage. But you are rigid. You hesitate because you are waiting for permission."

"I don't need permission."

"Then proof it."

He takes my chin in his hand, tilting my head back. The grip is firm, commanding. It forces me to expose my throat.

"Say yes," he commands. "Agree to the terms. My boat. My lead. Your badge."

"And if I say no?"

"Then I leave. And you sit here with your frozen peas and your dead partner's file until the guilt eats you alive."

The truth of it is a physical blow. He's right. Without him, I'm just a woman screaming at a building that won't burn.

I look into his eyes. There is no softness there, no promise of safety. There is only the brutally honest offer of shared violence. He is offering me the one thing no one else has: the capacity to hurt the people who hurt Jack.

The pull is irresistible. It's the seduction of absolute competence. I am tired of being the only one holding the line. I want to let the monster off the leash. I want to run with the wolf.

"Fine," I whisper.

"Say it."

"Yes."

His thumb brushes my lower lip, a rough caress that feels more like a brand. His gaze drops to my mouth, heavy and possessive. For a second, the air between us crackles, thick enough to choke on. I want him to kiss me. I want him to erase the grief with the same violence he uses to erase his enemies.

But he doesn't.

He pulls back, the cold air rushing into the space between us.

"Pack a bag," he says, buttoning his coat. "Waterproof gear. Long guns. No pistols. We leave in twenty minutes."

He turns and walks toward the door.

"Dario."

He pauses, hand on the knob.

"If you cross me... if this is a trap..."

He looks over his shoulder. The shadows carve his face into a mask of stone.

"If I wanted to trap you, *tesoro*, you wouldn't be standing."

The lock clicks. The door opens and closes.

I am alone in the silence of my apartment.

My hands are shaking. not from fear, but from the sudden, terrifying clarity of what I've just done. I have signed a blood contract with the devil.

I walk to the bedroom and pull my tactical duffel from the closet. I pack the Kevlar. I pack the rifle.

I'm done waiting for permission.

Let's go find some ghosts.

Chapter Six

CARBON AND BONE

The *Vesuvius* is not a pleasure craft. It is a predator painted black, idling in a slip at the darkest edge of the marina. There is no chrome, no white leather, no champagne fridge. It is sixty feet of radar-absorbent composite and engines tuned for smuggling, sitting low in the water like a panther waiting to pounce.

Rain hammers against the hull as I step from the dock to the deck. The fiberglass is slick under my boots. The air tastes of diesel, salt, and the low-pressure ozone of the incoming storm.

Dario does not wait for me. He is already inside the main cabin, the door sliding shut behind me to cut off the sound of the wind.

The silence here is heavy, pressurized. The only illumination comes from red tactical lights running along the floorboards, designed to preserve night vision. It turns the cabin into a developing room, stripping the world of color and leaving only shadows and intent.

"You're late," Dario says.

He stands by a bolted-down steel table in the center of the cabin. A black Pelican case lies open before him, revealing a nest of dark foam and darker metal.

"Traffic was murder," I say, dropping my duffel bag on a bench. "Or it would have been, if I hadn't used the siren."

He doesn't look up. He is field-stripping a rifle, his hands moving with a fluid, terrifying competence. *Click. Snap. Slide.* The sounds are rhythmic, a percussion of violence that settles my nerves better than any whiskey could.

I walk to the table. The smell of high-grade gun oil hits me—a scent that has always meant *work*.

"What are we carrying?" I ask.

"HK416s," he says, sliding a bolt carrier group back into place. "Suppressors. Subsonic ammunition. We aren't going there to make noise, Agent. We are going to excise a tumor."

I pick up the second rifle from the case. It is heavy, cold, and beautifully balanced. I check the chamber, verify the feed ramp is polished, and rack the charging handle. The spring tension is stiff, new.

"These aren't cartel issue," I note. "And they aren't military surplus."

"I have friends in Oberndorf who prefer cash to paperwork."

He finally looks at me. The red light casts his face in demonic relief, deepening the hollows under his cheekbones and turning his eyes into black pits. He watches me handle the weapon, his gaze tracking my fingers as I check the safety selector.

"You are comfortable with that platform?" he asks.

"I qualified expert three years running."

"Paper targets don't shoot back."

"Neither did the six men in your club," I counter. "And they're just as dead."

A corner of his mouth lifts. It is a dark, approving shape. "Fair enough."

He turns away to grab a tactical vest from the bench. He begins to unbutton his shirt.

I should look away. I should focus on loading the magazines arranged in precise rows on the table.

I don't.

He strips the ruined dress shirt off, tossing it into a corner. My mouth goes dry, a sudden drought that has nothing to do with the recycled air.

Dario Ferri is built like a siege engine. In the suit, he was imposing; stripped to the waist, he is overwhelming. His torso is a landscape of violence—slabs of pectoral muscle hard enough to crack bone, tapering down to a stomach ridged with dense, functional power. But it's his arms that hold me hostage. As he reaches for a black combat shirt, the muscles in his forearms shift and coil like steel cables under bronze skin. Thick veins rope over his biceps, feeding the machine. He is scarred, a map of past wars carved into his flesh—a burn on his ribs, a jagged white line tracing over his deltoid, the pucker of an old bullet wound near his collarbone.

He is not beautiful in the way models are beautiful. He is beautiful in the way a loaded weapon is beautiful. He is potential energy waiting for a trigger. The sheer, kinetic reality of him makes the air in the cabin feel thin. I want to trace the path of that scar on his shoulder. I want to know if his skin is as hot as the heat radiating off him suggests. It is a biological imperative, a thirst spiking in my blood—the urge to align myself with the apex predator in the room.

He pulls the combat shirt over his head, hiding the show. The fabric clings to him, outlining the heavy musculature of his shoulders.

He catches me staring. He doesn't preen. He doesn't smile. He just holds my gaze, his eyes dark with knowledge. He knows exactly what he is. And he knows I see it.

"Focus, *tesoro*," he rumbles. "Lust is a distraction. Survival is a discipline."

Heat flushes my neck. "I was checking for injuries."

"You were checking my specs." He picks up the plate carrier. "Turn around."

I bristle. "I can dress myself."

"Turn around."

The command is absolute. My body obeys before my brain can argue. I turn my back to him.

He slides the heavy Kevlar vest over my head. The weight settles on my shoulders, a familiar burden. He steps in close, his chest brushing my back. The heat coming off him is a furnace.

"Lift your arms," he murmurs near my ear.

I comply. His hands move to the side straps. He doesn't just buckle them; he cinches them. He pulls the velcro tight, compressing my ribs, locking me into the armor. His knuckles graze the sensitive skin of my side, sending a jolt of electricity straight to my spine.

"Too loose," he criticizes, his voice a low vibration against my shoulder blades. "If you take a round to the ceramic, the backface deformation will break your ribs if the vest isn't a second skin."

He jerks the straps tighter. It knocks the wind out of me for a second. I am encased in ceramic and nylon, but I have never felt more exposed.

He moves to the front, stepping around me. He checks the fit, his hands running over the strike face of the plate, then up to the shoulder releases. It is intimate. It is the intimacy of the armory, of the gladiator pit. He is ensuring I survive, not because he loves me, but because I am his wingman.

"Comfortable?" he asks.

"I can breathe," I gasp. "Barely."

"Good. Breathing is a luxury. Bleeding is the alternative."

He steps back, breaking the field of gravity between us. He picks up his own vest and shrugs it on with practiced ease, securing it in seconds.

He looks at me then—really looks at me. I am wearing black cargo pants, combat boots, and a tactical vest stamped with *FEDERAL AGENT* on the velcro patch.

He reaches out and rips the patch off. The sound of tearing velcro is loud in the quiet cabin.

"Hey!"

"No badges," he says, tossing the patch onto the table. "Tonight, you answer to no agency. Tonight, you are not the law. You are the consequence."

He hands me a suppressor.

"Screw this on. Check the alignment. If you get a baffle strike, you lose a hand."

I take the cold cylinder. My hands are shaking, just a little. Not from fear, but from the adrenaline cocktail flooding my system. The silence in the room is a liar. It promises safety, whispering that I could just stay here, curl into the sheets of a normal life, and let the world burn without me. But the hunger is hotter.

It burns beneath my ribs, a jagged, desperate thing. I don't want safety; I want the quiet that comes after the scream. I want the heavy yoke of this bureaucracy snapped in two, even if the shrapnel cuts me. I crave the end of this waiting more than I value my own skin.

I thread the suppressor onto the barrel. *Twist. Twist. Lock.*

"We are going to kill them," I say. It isn't a question.

Dario loads a magazine into his rifle and slaps the bottom to seat it.

"We are going to burn it down," he corrects. "All of it."

He moves to the cockpit, flicking a bank of switches overhead. The engines rumble to life, a deep, throaty growl that vibrates through the deck plates and up into my bones. The red lights flicker, then stabilize.

"Cast off the stern line," he orders.

I move to the rear deck. The rain soaks me instantly, plastering my hair to my face. I untie the heavy rope and toss it onto the dock. We are adrift.

I step back inside, locking the hatch against the storm.

Dario pushes the throttles forward. The *Vesuvius* surges, the bow rising as it cuts through the black water of the harbor.

We slip past the breakwater, leaving the lights of San Diego behind. Ahead, there is only the Pacific Ocean, vast and indifferent, and the darkness where monsters hide.

I grip the rifle. I watch Dario's profile illuminated by the green glow of the radar screen. He looks like Charon piloting the ferry across the Styx.

I am not a passenger. I am holding a rifle.

"Course set," he says over the hum of the engines. "Two hours to the border. Four to the island."

"I'm ready."

He glances at me. The shadows hide his eyes, but I hear the grim satisfaction in his voice.

"Then try to sleep, Merritt. It's the last rest you'll get."

I sit on the bench, the rifle across my knees. I don't sleep. I watch the wake of the boat churn the black water into white foam, and I wait for the fire.

CHAPTER SEVEN

THE QUIET AND THE KILL

The United States ends not with a wall, but with a sudden, suffocating absence of light.

San Diego is a smoldering ember on the horizon behind us, a haze of orange pollution and wasted electricity. Ahead, the Pacific is a black throat waiting to swallow us whole.

The *Vesuvius* cuts through the swells with the violence of a knife fight. There is no comfort here. The hull slams against the water, a rhythmic car crash that vibrates through the soles of my boots and settles in my teeth. I grip the handrail of the cockpit, my knuckles bleached white.

We just crossed the maritime boundary.

I know the coordinates by heart. I've enforced them for fifteen years. I've arrested men for crossing this invisible line with a trunk full of fentanyl or a hull full of desperate souls. That line was my religion. It was the distinction between order and chaos, between the righteous and the damned.

Tonight, I crossed it without blinking. I didn't radio it in. I didn't log a float plan. I just stood here and watched the GPS numbers tick over, officially becoming a ghost.

"Stop staring at the chart," Dario says.

He stands at the helm, bathed in the sickly green glow of the radar and navigation arrays. One hand rests lightly on the throttle, the other on the wheel. He pilots the boat with the same terrifying, relaxed competence he uses to break men's fingers. He doesn't look at the sea; he feels it.

"I'm checking our bearing," I say, my voice sounding thin over the roar of the twin diesels.

"Our bearing is South-Southwest. The bearing isn't bothering you. The jurisdiction is."

He turns his head. The shadows in the cabin carve his face into hard, predatory angles. He sees too much. It's annoying.

"I'm a federal agent, Dario. Leaving my jurisdiction with a trunk full of illegal suppressors and a known felon tends to itch."

"Former federal agent," he corrects. "The moment we crossed that line, your badge became a piece of tin. Out here, there is no due process. There is only the food chain."

"And where are we on that chain?"

He taps the throttle, pushing the engines harder. The boat leaps, airborne for a split second before slamming down into a trough. Spray lashes the windshield.

"We are the things with teeth, Merritt. Act like it."

I turn away from him, moving to the bench where my gear sits. I need to do something with my hands. If I don't, I'll start shaking, and I refuse to let him see me shake.

I pick up the HK416. I've checked it three times. I check it a fourth. I drop the magazine, rack the charging handle, and inspect the chamber. The brass glints, clean and deadly.

This rifle is unregistered. Ghost gun. If I use it, there is no ballistics match. No paper trail.

Jack would hate this. Jack believed in the paperwork. He believed that if you filled out the forms correctly, the world made sense.

They cut him apart while he was alive.

The thought flashes hot and bright, searing away the doubt. Paperwork didn't save Jack. The law didn't stop the knife.

I slam the magazine back into the well. The sound is a sharp crack, like a gavel coming down.

"Coffee," Dario says.

I look up. He's holding out a steel thermos. He hasn't left the wheel, but he's watching me in the reflection of the glass.

I take it. The metal is warm. I unscrew the cap and drink. Black. Bitter. Strong enough to strip paint. The caffeine hits my bloodstream like a slap.

"You said four hours," I say, wiping my mouth.

"The storm is pushing the swell. Make it five."

"Tell me about the island."

"I gave you the file."

"I want to hear it from you. The file lists structures and guard rotations. I want to know what the satellite photos don't show."

Dario engages the autopilot. He steps away from the console, the green light washing off him, replaced by the dim red tactical glow of the cabin. He moves into my space. The cabin is small. He makes it smaller.

He leans against the bulkhead, crossing his arms over his chest. The movement pulls the black fabric of his combat shirt tight against his biceps.

"The photos don't show the smell," he says quietly.

"What smell?"

"Despair. And bleach." His jaw works, a muscle bunching tight. "This faction... they are not businessmen. They are zealots. They believe pain purifies the soul. They take the boys to the breaking yards. They starve them, drug them, force them to kill animals. By the time they are done, the boy is gone. Only the soldier remains."

"And the girls?"

The temperature in the cabin drops. Dario looks past me, staring at the black glass of the porthole. For a second, the mask of the Capo slips. I don't see the monster. I see a man looking at a grave.

"The girls are currency," he rasps. "They are broken differently. They are taught that their only value is submission. That their bodies are not their own."

He pushes off the wall, pacing two steps to the left, then back. A caged tiger.

"I don't deal in flesh, Merritt. I sell vice. Gambling. Booze. Protection. Things people choose. But this?" He gestures to the south. "This is a sickness."

"Is that why you're helping me?" I ask. "Because it's bad for business?"

He stops. He looks down at me. His eyes are black holes, absorbing the red light.

"I had a sister," he says.

The words hang in the air, heavier than the humidity.

I freeze. The dossier didn't mention a sister. It mentioned a dead father, a mother in a care home in Sicily. No siblings.

"Maria," he says. The name sounds foreign on his tongue, like a prayer he hasn't said in years. "She was sixteen. She wanted to be a teacher. She had a laugh that could make you forget you were poor."

He walks to the bench and sits down next to me. Close. His knee brushes mine. The heat coming off him is a distraction I can't afford, but I lean into it anyway.

"What happened to her?"

"I was young. Just starting to make a name for myself in the families. I thought I was untouchable." He looks at his hands—hands that have killed men, hands that are currently resting on his thighs, unclenched but ready. "A rival crew took her. To teach me a lesson. To show me that I was not the king I thought I was."

My stomach turns over. "Dario..."

"They kept her for three days." His voice is devoid of inflection, which makes it worse. It is the flat tone of someone reading a casualty report. "When I found her... she was broken. Not just her body. Her mind. She couldn't speak. She couldn't look at me."

He turns to me. The pain in his eyes is ancient, calcified.

"She took her own life a year later. She couldn't live with the ghosts."

He reaches out, his hand hovering near my face before his fingers brush a stray lock of hair behind my ear. The touch is startlingly gentle, at odds with the violence of his story.

"I burned that crew to ash," he whispers. "I killed every man who touched her. I killed the men who gave the order. I killed their drivers. But it didn't bring her back."

"Vengeance never does," I say.

"No. But it quiets the noise."

His thumb traces the line of my jaw. My breath hitches. We are two feet apart, but the distance feels nonexistent. We are bound by the dead. Jack. Maria. The people we failed to save.

"That island," he says, his gaze dropping to my mouth. "It is full of Marias. And the men guarding them... they are the same men who took her. Different faces. Same rot."

"Then we kill them," I say. The words are hard, sharp stones in my mouth. "We kill them all."

Dario studies me. He is looking for flinching, for the softness of the government agent. He doesn't find it. He finds the jagged edges where the grief broke me.

"Yes," he agrees. "We will."

The boat lurches violently. A wave slams the port side, throwing me against him.

His arm goes around me instantly, anchoring me. His body is a wall of solid muscle. I grab his vest to steady myself. Our faces are inches apart.

I can smell the coffee on his breath, mixed with the salt air. I can feel the rapid hammer of his heart against my hand.

This is dangerous. This proximity. It's not just survival. It's acknowledgment. We are two predators sharing a cage, heading toward a slaughter. The adrenaline is already spiking, mixing with the grief to create a cocktail that tastes like lust.

I want to kiss him. I want to bury my hands in his hair and forget that I am about to commit murder. I want to feel something other than the cold.

Dario reads the intent in my eyes. His pupils dilate. His hand on my waist tightens, pulling me flush against him. The armor between us is a barrier, but I can feel the heat radiating through the ceramic plates.

"Merritt," he warns, his voice a low growl. "If you start this, we do not stop."

"I'm not asking you to stop."

He leans in. His lips brush the corner of my mouth. It's not a kiss; it's a question. A test.

"We are entering the kill box," he murmurs against my skin. "You need to be sharp. You need to be ice."

"I am ice."

"No." He pulls back a fraction, his dark eyes burning. "You are fire. You are burning alive, *tesoro*. I can feel it."

He releases me abruptly. The loss of contact leaves me cold.

He stands up and moves back to the helm. The moment is broken, shattered by the discipline that keeps him alive.

"Twenty miles out," he calls over his shoulder, his voice back to the command tone. "Get your gear. We go dark in ten."

I sit on the bench for a second, my heart racing. I touch my lips where he brushed them.

He's right. I am burning.

I stand up. I check the seal on my dry bag. I check the battery on my optics. I shove the feelings down into the black box where I keep Jack's memory.

I walk to the cockpit. The rain is lashing the glass now, turning the world into a blur of gray and black.

"Lights out," Dario orders.

He kills the running lights. The red glow in the cabin dies.

We are plunging into absolute darkness.

I step up beside him. I don't look at him. I look at the void ahead.

"I see the signature," I say, pointing to a faint blip on the radar.

"That's them," Dario confirms. "Isla de la Sangre."

He pulls the throttles back. The roar of the engines drops to a sinister purr. We are prowling now.

"Ready?" he asks.

I rack the slide on the rifle again, just to hear the sound. It is the only honest thing left in the world.

"Let's go to work."

*

The transition from the boat to the Zodiac is an exercise in misery.

The ocean is angry. The waves are six-foot walls of black water that try to smash the rubber raft against the hull of the *Vesuvius*. Cold spray soaks me instantly, finding the gaps in my collar, running down my spine like ice water. But the discomfort is distant, irrelevant.

I am in the zone.

The noise of the world—the wind, the waves, the shout of my own doubts—fades into a dull hum. My focus narrows to the immediate: The grip of the paddle. The rhythm of Dario's stroke in front of me. The dark shape of the island looming out of the mist like the spine of a submerged leviathan.

We beach the Zodiac in a small cove on the north side, hidden by jagged rocks that tear at the water.

We move fast. We drag the raft up the sand, covering it with drag nets and brush. We are silent. We don't need words. We have the plan.

Infil. Recon. Destroy. Exfil.

Dario takes point. He moves through the scrub brush with an eerie silence for a man of his size. He is a shadow detach from the night. I follow in his wake, stepping where he steps, my rifle up, scanning the cliffs above.

The air here is different. It's heavy. Clammy. It smells of rotting kelp and something sweeter, something copper-tangy.

Old blood.

We reach the tree line. Dario raises a fist. I freeze, dropping to one knee in the wet sand.

He signals: *Two tangos. Twelve o'clock. High ground.*

I bring my scope up. The night vision washes the world in green phosphor.

There they are. Two guards patrolling the ridge. They are smoking cigarettes, the cherry embers glowing bright in the optic. They look relaxed. They are laughing.

They have no idea the reapers are at the gate.

Dario looks back at me. He points to the left guard, then points to himself. He points to the right guard, then to me.

On my count.

I adjust my aim. The crosshair settles on the guard's chest. I breathe out, emptying my lungs, finding the pause between heartbeats.

This is it. The threshold.

If I pull this trigger, I am no longer a federal agent. I am an assassin. I am the vigilante the Director warned me about.

I look at the guard. He is young. Maybe twenty. Just a kid with a rifle and a bad set of choices.

Then I think of the dog in the cage. I think of Jack, screaming while they cut him. I think of the girls Dario described, broken and hollowed out.

The hesitation evaporates.

Dario holds up three fingers.

Two.

One.

My finger tightens. The rifle bucks against my shoulder. The suppressed *pfft* is swallowed by the sound of the surf.

The guard on the right drops.

Dario's target falls a split second later.

We move.

We scramble up the rocks, boots seeking purchase on the slick stone. We reach the bodies. I check mine. Dead before he hit the ground.

Dario drags the bodies into the brush. He rifles through their pockets, grabbing a radio and a key card.

He turns to me. His face is streaked with mud and rain. He looks terrifying. He looks right.

"Welcome to the island, *tesoro*," he whispers.

I look down at the compound spread out in the valley below. A cluster of concrete buildings surrounded by high fences and razor wire. A church spire rises in the center, a perverse monument overlooking the cages.

I feel a cold, hard knot form in my stomach. It's not fear. It's hate. Pure, crystalline hate.

"Lead the way," I say.

We descend into the dark. The water behind us is black. The way back is closed.

The only way out is through the fire.

CHAPTER EIGHT

THE QUIET AND THE HUNGER

The safehouse smells of dry rot, salt, and the ghosts of bad men.

It's a concrete block perched on a crumbling bluff south of Ensenada, invisible from the road and indistinguishable from the rocks to the sea. Inside, it is sparse. A single mattress on a frame that rusts in the salty air. A table scarred by knife blades. A generator humming low and angry in the corner.

I drop the duffel bag on the floor. My knees hit the concrete a second later.

It isn't a collapse. It's a tactical changing of levels, or that's what I tell myself. But the floor doesn't stop moving. The boat ride is still in my inner ear, the violent pitch and roll of the black ocean translating into a phantom sway that makes the room tilt.

"Breathe," Dario says.

He locks the heavy steel door. Three bolts. *Click. Click. Click.* The sound is final. We are sealed in.

"I'm fine," I say. My voice sounds like it's coming from someone else—someone made of glass.

"You are shaking."

He walks past me to the table. He starts unloading the gear, his movements precise, efficient. Rifle. Magazines. The heavy breaching charges. He treats the instruments of death with more reverence than a priest treats a chalice.

I force myself up. My legs feel like lead pipe, heavy and unbending. I walk to the small kitchenette sink and turn the tap. Brown water spits out, then clears. I splash it on my face. It's cold enough to hurt.

I look at my reflection in the cracked mirror. My eyes are hollowed out. Dark bruises bloom under the skin, evidence of the lack of sleep, the stress, the crushing weight of the badge I ripped off my chest. I look like a woman who has been hunting monsters so long she forgot how to be human.

Jack is dead. The girls are in cages. The Director is probably drafting my arrest warrant.

"Stop it," Dario says.

I turn. He isn't looking at the weapons anymore. He's leaning against the table, his arms crossed over that massive chest, watching me.

"Stop what?"

"Stop thinking. I can hear the gears grinding from here. You are trying to solve the equation, Merritt. There is no equation. There is only the target."

"I need to review the schematics again. If we hit the generator room first, we cut their comms, but we risk—"

"No."

He pushes off the table. He crosses the room in two strides. He doesn't stop until he is in my personal space, consuming the air, blocking out the light.

"We go in at 0300. That is six hours from now. If you go into that breach with your mind spinning like a centrifuge, you will die. And worse, you will get me killed."

"I don't know how to turn it off," I whisper. The admission tastes like ash. "The noise... it never stops."

"I know."

He reaches out. His hand wraps around the back of my neck. His thumb presses into the pulse point below my ear. His skin is rough, calloused from years of gripping gun stocks and steering wheels, but his touch is possessive. Grounding.

"You carry the weight of the world, *tesoro*. The law. The victims. The dead partner. It is too much for one spine."

His thumb strokes the sensitive skin of my throat. My breath hitches. The sensation sends a jolt of electricity straight down my center, bypassing my brain entirely.

"Let me take it," he says. His voice drops, becoming a low rumble that vibrates through his chest and into mine. "Just for tonight. Let me carry the weight."

"Dario..."

"Kneel."

The command is soft, but it hits me with the force of a physical blow.

My eyes widen. I look up at him. I expect to see mockery, or the cruel arrogance of the mobster. I see neither. I see a dark, terrible focus. I see a man who understands that control is a burden, and surrender is a gift.

My knees weaken, not from exhaustion this time, but from a sudden, liquid heat that pools in my belly. It is a terrifying impulse—the urge to obey. To let go of the reins. To stop being Special Agent Gage and just be... held.

I sink down.

The concrete is cold through my tactical pants. I kneel between his boots, looking up at him. From this angle, he is a monolith. A dark god of violence and structure.

"Good," he murmurs.

His hand leaves my neck. He tangles his fingers in my hair, gripping tight enough to pull my scalp, forcing my head back. I expose my throat to him. It is the ultimate vulnerability. I am offering him the softest part of me, the place where the lifeblood runs closest to the surface.

He studies my face. He traces the line of my jaw with his eyes.

"You are so loud," he whispers. "Always analyzing. Always fighting. Be quiet now."

He uses his grip on my hair to guide me forward. I rest my forehead against his thigh. The denim of his jeans is rough against my skin. Underneath, his muscle is hard as iron. I smell the gun oil, the sea salt, and the musk of a man who has been working. It is intoxicating.

"Unbutton them," he orders.

I don't ask who or what. I know. My hands shake as I reach for the button of my pants. I fumble.

"Slowly," he corrects. "There is no rush. The world has stopped."

I undo the button. The zipper hisses down. I shove the heavy fabric down my hips, feeling the cool air of the safehouse on my skin. I am exposed. I am vulnerable.

And for the first time in weeks, the noise in my head stops.

There is no Director. No cartel. No Jack. There is only the man standing above me and the heat radiating from his body.

Dario shifts. He steps back, creating space. He points to the heavy wooden chair in the corner of the room.

"Sit."

I crawl to it. I don't stand. I move on my hands and knees across the cold floor. It feels primal. It feels right. I reach the chair and pull myself up, sitting on the edge, my legs spread, my pants tangled around my ankles.

He watches me. His eyes are black fire. He is drinking me in, not with the lecherous gaze of the men I arrest, but with the appreciation of a craftsman looking at a fine tool, or a devotee looking at an icon.

He walks to me. He drops to his knees.

The change in elevation shocks me. Dario Ferri does not kneel. He makes others kneel. But here he is, between my legs, his shoulders broad enough to block out the rest of the room.

He places his hands on my thighs. His thumbs press into the muscle, parting me wider. He is claiming territory.

"You belong to the government nine days out of ten," he says, his voice rough. "But tonight, in this room, you are mine."

"Yours," I gasp. The word is a plea.

He leans forward. His breath ghosting over me is hot, moist heat against sensitive flesh. I flinch, my hips bucking involuntarily.

"Still," he commands. His grip on my thighs tightens, anchoring me.

Then he tastes me.

It is not tentative. It is a conquest. His tongue is broad, flat, and skilled. He drags it slowly from bottom to top, a long, languid stroke that steals the air from the room.

My head falls back against the wood of the chair. A sound tears out of my throat—half sob, half moan. My hands find his shoulders, grabbing the fabric of his black shirt, trying to find purchase as the world tilts on its axis.

He doesn't stop. He doesn't tease. He devours.

He works with a rhythmic, punishing consistency. He finds the bundle of nerves hidden under the hood and circles it, relentlessly. It is overwhelming. It is too much and not enough.

"Dario," I beg. "Please."

He ignores me. He is a man of code, and right now, his code is my pleasure. He uses his tongue to flicker, rapid and light, then follows it with the suction of his mouth, hard and demanding.

My vision blurs. The ceiling of the safehouse dissolves into a haze of gray. Every nerve ending in my body is firing at once, screaming for release. The tension coils in my belly, a tight, hot spring winding tighter and tighter.

He senses it. Of course he does. He deals in pressure.

He slides two fingers inside me.

I cry out. The stretch is full, invasive, perfect. He curls them, beckoning, hitting the spot deep inside that makes my toes curl. He establishes a rhythm—his tongue against the clitoris, his fingers thrusting inside.

It is a dual assault. He is taking me apart.

"Look at me," he growls against my skin.

I force my eyes open. It takes every ounce of will I have left.

He looks up. His face is wet with me. His beard is rough, grazing my inner thighs. His eyes are dilated, black pits of obsession. He looks demonic. He looks holy.

"Let go, Merritt. Give it to me."

The command shatters the last of my resistance.

The spring snaps.

It starts in my core, a nuclear chain reaction. The pleasure hits me like a physical wave, cresting and crashing over my head. I arch off the chair, screaming his name. My body clamps down on his fingers, pulsing, milking.

He drinks it all. He stays with me through every spasm, his tongue working, his hands holding my hips so I don't fall, absorbing my tremors into his own body. He worships the shuddering wreck of me until I am completely empty, until I am nothing but breath and sweat and silence.

I collapse back against the chair. My lungs burn for air. My heart hammers a frantic rhythm against my ribs, but it is a clean rhythm. The panic is gone. The darkness is gone.

Dario pulls back slowly. He rests his forehead against my knee for a moment, his breathing heavy, ragged.

Then he stands.

He wipes his mouth with the back of his hand. He looks down at me, sprawled and undone on the chair.

He picks me up.

He lifts me easily, as if I weigh nothing, and carries me to the mattress in the corner. He lays me down. He doesn't join me. He pulls the scratchy wool blanket over me, tucking it around my shoulders with a jarring tenderness.

"Sleep," he says. "I will take the first watch."

I look at him. He is back in the center of the room, reloading a magazine. The monster is back in the cage, but the door is unlocked.

I close my eyes. For the first time in years, I don't dream of the dead. I dream of fire.

CHAPTER NINE

THE ARCHITECTURE OF SILENCE

The compound does not look like a slaughterhouse. It looks like a tech startup built by a paranoid billionaire.

Brushed steel walls replace the rotting wood of the jungle shacks we passed earlier. The floors are polished concrete, slick and gray, reflecting the recessed lighting that hums with a headache-inducing frequency. The air is scrubbed clean, filtered through high-efficiency particulate arrestors until it smells of absolutely nothing. No rot. No salt. Just the terrifying sterility of intent.

Dario moves ahead of me. He is a shadow sliding across the gray, his boots making no sound. He signals *hold* with a closed fist.

I stop. My shoulder presses against the cold metal of a junction box. The HK416 is heavy in my hands, a dead weight that usually brings comfort, but here, in this antiseptic hall, it feels primitive. We are hunting ghosts in a machine.

Dario checks the corner. He nods. *Clear.*

We push forward. The surveillance Intel from the boat was wrong. This isn't just a holding facility. It's a laboratory.

We pass rooms behind safety glass. Empty. Clean. But the drains in the center of the floors are stained a dark, rusty brown that no amount of bleach can lift.

Dario swipes the key card we took from the guard at the beach. The light on the heavy door at the end of the hall blinks green. The mag-lock disengages with a heavy *thud*.

He pushes it open.

The sound hits us first.

It isn't screaming. Screaming I could handle. Screaming is human. This is worse. It is a recorded loop, a synthesized voice reciting the *Pater Noster* in a monotone, rhythmic cadence, layered over a high-pitched frequency that burrows straight into the jagged edges of my teeth.

...on earth as it is in heaven. Give us this day...

We step inside. It's the control center.

Banks of monitors line the far wall, bathing the room in a sickly, phosphor-green glow. The air is freezing, kept sub-zero to protect the servers humming in the racks to our left.

I walk to the console. My boots feel too loud. My heart feels too loud.

"Look," Dario says. His voice is a grind of gravel, barely audible over the server hum.

I look at the screens.

The feed is black and white, grainy night vision. It cycles through the cages.

Cage 1: A boy, maybe twelve, curled in a fetal ball on a concrete floor. He is naked. He is shivering so violently the pixels blur.

Cage 2: A girl. Older. She is standing perfectly still, staring at a speaker mounted on the wall, her lips moving in time with the recorded prayer. Her eyes are wide, unblinking, devoid of anything resembling a soul.

Cage 3: Empty. Just a bucket and a drain.

"They're conditioning them," I whisper. The realization makes my stomach turn over. "Sleep deprivation. Auditory driving. It's MKUltra tactics adapted for the cartel."

Dario rips a cable out of the console. One of the screens goes black. He doesn't look at the monitors. He looks at the glass partition separating the control room from the observation deck below.

"Not just the cartel," he says.

I follow his gaze. On the desk, next to the keyboard, is a stack of shipping manifests. I pick one up. The logo at the top is familiar. *Vance Global Logistics.*

The paper crinkles in my grip.

Julian. My brother-in-law. The politician who swore he was cleaning up the ports. The man whose funeral I attended three weeks ago.

"He wasn't fighting them," I say. The words taste like copper. "He was the transport."

"He was the pipeline," Dario corrects.

He steps closer to me. The green light casts deep shadows across his face, turning the scars into canyons. He looks like a demon unleashed in a church, furious and holy all at once.

"This is the ledger," he says, pointing to the server racks. "The names of the buyers. The auction dates. The prices for the..." He stops. He cannot say the word *children*. "For the inventory."

The synthesized voice drones on. ...*forgive us our trespasses*...

I can't breathe. The room is shrinking. The sterility, the cold, the monotonous prayer—it's pressing against my skull. I'm an agent of the state. I deal in statutes and warrants. I build cases. I don't know how to process a factory designed to uninstall humanity from a child.

"Merritt."

Dario's voice is sharp. A command.

I look at him.

He's blocked my view of the monitors. He stands between me and the horror, a wall of black tactical gear and brute force.

And God, the sight of him is the only thing anchoring me to the earth.

He has discarded the heavy plate carrier, stripped down to the black combat shirt that clings to him like second skin. The fabric strains across the expanse of his chest, unable to hide the absolute, kinetic density of him. His deltoids are boulders tailored into human shape, intersected by the thick, functional straps of his weapon sling.

My gaze drops to his hands. They are resting on the console, knuckles white as he grips the edge. They are large, scarred hands. Hands that have killed. Hands that have broken bones. Hands that stripped a rifle in the dark with the grace of a pianist.

A sudden, violent thirst spikes in my blood. It's not rational. It's biological. It's the lizard brain screaming that death is in the room, and I need to align myself with the strongest thing here to survive it. I need to know that *this* body—this massive, warm, violent engine—is on my side.

"I need..." My voice cracks. I don't know what I need. I need to burn this place down. I need to forget the dead look in that girl's eyes.

Dario sees it. He reads the panic fracturing my iris.

He moves.

He doesn't step back. He steps *in*. He crowds me against the server rack. The metal bites into my lower back, cold and hard, but his body is a furnace pressing against my front.

"Don't look at them," he growls.

The prayer from the speakers seems to get louder. *...lead us not into temptation...*

"I can hear them," I gasp. "Dario, the sound—"

"Listen to me."

He gripping my hips. His fingers dig into the tactical belt, hauling me up. I scramble for purchase, my boots sliding on the polished floor until I am sitting on the edge of the server housing, my legs wrapping around his waist instinctively.

"Focus on me," he orders.

He drops to his knees.

The movement is so sudden, so submissive yet dominating, that the air leaves my lungs. He forces my legs wider, his broad shoulders pushing my thighs apart until the ache in my hips is the only signal my brain can process.

He doesn't ask. He doesn't hesitate. He acts with the same ruthless efficiency he uses to silence a room.

His hands grip the back of my thighs, anchoring me, and he buries his face against me.

The tactical pants are a barrier he doesn't tolerate. He shoves the fabric aside, tearing a seam in his haste. The sound of ripping cloth is a violent punctuation mark in the quiet room.

Then, his mouth is on me.

The shock of it nearly throws me off the rack. It is hot, wet, and incredibly firm.

"Dario—"

He grunts, a vibration against my most sensitive skin, and uses his tongue.

It is a claiming. He licks long and slow, a heavy stroke from bottom to top that drags a moan from my throat. The sound destroys the rhythm of the recorded prayer.

...deliver us from evil...

His tongue finds the hooded nerve, and the world narrows down to that single point of contact. He is relentless. He knows exactly how to move, how to apply pressure. He treats my pleasure like a mission objective—something to be secured with lethal precision.

I weave my fingers into his hair. It's thick, dark, and damp with sweat. I pull, trying to anchor myself, trying to leverage the sensation that is rapidly spiraling out of control.

He hums against me, a low, guttural sound of approval as my hips buck.

The drone of the speakers fades. The voice reciting scripture becomes background noise, drowned out by the harsh, wet sound of his mouth working, the ragged intake of his breath, and the blood rushing in my ears like a breaking tide.

He isn't gentle. There is no room for gentleness in a place like this. He uses his teeth, a light graze that sends a jolt of electricity straight to my spine, followed by the soothing, suctioning heat of his lips. He sucks hard, drawing me out, demanding everything I have.

He is drinking the panic out of me. He is replacing the cold horror of the screens with the blistering heat of his devotion.

"Dario, please," I beg, my head falling back, hitting the metal server cage. "I'm close. I'm—"

He doesn't stop. He speeds up. His tongue flickers, rapid-fire, a weaponized rhythm. He slides a finger inside me, stretching, filling, curling to hit the internal trigger while his mouth destroys the external one.

It's too much. It's sensory overload. The smell of gun oil, the hum of the servers, the taste of ozone, and the overwhelming, consuming pressure of him.

I shatter.

It rips through me, a white-hot detonation that starts in my belly and blows out my extremities. I clamp my legs around his head, trapping him, sobbing his name. I am shaking apart, stripped of the Shield, stripped of the badge, reduced to raw nerve and reflex.

He stays with me. He absorbs every tremor. He drinks the release, licking me clean, soothing the hypersensitive flesh until the spasms subside into a dull, throbbing glow.

He rests his forehead against my thigh for a moment, his breathing heavy, laboring like a bellows.

The silence returns.

But it's different now. The recorded prayer is still playing, but it has lost its power. It's just noise. The horror is still on the screens, but I am no longer paralyzed by it. I am ground down and built back up. I am flesh and blood.

Dario stands up.

He towers over me, wiping his mouth with the back of his hand. His eyes are black holes, dilated and dangerous. He looks at me—disheveled, flushed, sitting on a server rack in a house of horrors—and nods once.

"Better?" he asks roughly.

"Yes." My voice is steady. The shake is gone.

I slide off the rack. My legs are weak, but my resolve is iron. I pull my pants up. I fasten my belt. I zip the fly.

Zzzzzzt.

The sound is sharp. Definitive. It sounds exactly like the slide of a pistol racking a round into the chamber.

Dario turns to the console. He pulls a small incendiary charge from his vest.

"Good," he says. He sets the timer for ten minutes. "Grab the hard drives. We're leaving."

"And the broadcast?" I ask, looking at the screens one last time.

Dario draws his knife. He jams it into the speaker mounted on the wall. The praying voice dies with a static screech.

" canceled," he says.

I shoulder my rifle. The weight feels good now. It feels like an answer.

"Let's go get the girls," I say.

We walk out of the room. We don't sneak this time. We hunt.

CHAPTER TEN
CONCRETE ANGELS, CORPORATE DEVILS

The hallway beyond the server room does not smell like a prison. It smells like a cathedral.

Frankincense, heavy and cloying, hangs in the recirculated air, fighting a losing war against the copper tang of old blood. My boots make no sound on the polished concrete. Beside me, Dario moves with the lethal fluidity of a great white shark in deep water. The black combat shirt clings to his sweat-dampened back, the muscle beneath shifting as he clears the corners.

Ten minutes ago, I was wrapped around him, unraveling in the dark. Now, the rifle stock welds to my shoulder, a familiar extension of my body. The transition should be jarring. It isn't. The line between sex and violence has always been thin for people like us—both are desperate confirmations of life in the face of the void.

We reach a heavy blast door. No key card reader. Just a wheel valve.

Dario holsters his pistol and grips the wheel. He looks at me. His eyes are hard, stripped of the heat that burned me alive moments ago.

"On the other side," he whispers, his voice a low grind of gravel, "there is no law. Do you understand?"

"Open it."

He twists the wheel. The mechanism groans—metal shearing against metal. He shoves the door outward.

We step into the heart of the machine.

It's an observation gallery. Below us, through unparalleled sheets of bulletproof glass, lies a cavernous retrofitted warehouse. The scale of it punches the air from my lungs. It isn't a dungeon. It is a dormitory of nightmares.

Rows of steel cages line the walls, stacked two high. Inside, small shapes huddle under thin solar blankets. In the center of the room, a massive wooden cross hangs suspended from the ceiling by chains. It is wrapped not in flowers, but in razor wire.

Beneath the cross, a man in a white linen suit stands over a kneeling figure.

I bring my optic up. The magnification clarifies the scene instantly.

The kneeling figure is a girl. Maybe fourteen. Her hair has been shaved off. She wears a white shift dress stained at the knees.

The man in the suit is holding a Bible in one hand and a cattle prod in the other.

"El Santo," Dario breathes. The name carries the weight of a curse. "I thought the Federales put a bullet in his head in Juarez three years ago."

"Government bullets don't stick when the target pays in dollars," I say. My finger hovers over the trigger guard. "He's the one running the conditioning?"

"He believes pain opens the mind to God. He breaks them down until they are empty vessels, then fills them with loyalty."

El Santo raises the prod. The blue arc of electricity snaps in the silence. He touches it to the girl's shoulder.

She doesn't scream. She squeezes her eyes shut and recites something. Her lips move in a frantic, rehearsed rhythm.

Submission.

The rage that flares in my chest is cold. It is absolute zero. This is what Jack died for. He didn't just stumble onto a drug route. He found a factory manufacturing slaves.

"We have to go down there," I say.

"Wait." Dario's hand clamps on my shoulder, stopping me. "Look at the perimeter. The shadows."

I adjust my scan. At first, I see nothing. Then, movement.

Men in tactical gear stand in the alcoves. They aren't wearing the mismatched fatigues of cartel enforcers. They wear matching gray digital camo. High-cut helmets. Night vision mounts. They hold suppressed MP5s at the low ready.

"That's not cartel," I murmur.

I focus on the patch on the nearest guard's shoulder. A sword bisecting a globe.

Paladin Global.

My stomach drops. "That's a PMC. American contractors."

"Mercenaries," Dario corrects.

"No. Paladin has government contracts. They provide security for embassies. For..." The realization hits me like a physical blow. "For the border processing centers."

The puzzle pieces slam together, forming a picture so grotesque I want to vomit. Julian didn't just transport them. He used his political connections to divert "lost" children from the border facilities straight into the hands of a private military company, who then sold them to a cartel cult for reprogramming.

It's a perfect circle of hell. Funded by taxpayers. Protected by bureaucracy.

"Your government at work?" Dario asks. He doesn't look at me. He is calculating angles, kill zones, exit routes.

"Not anymore." I flick the safety off. "Today, I resign."

"There are twelve shooters on the floor," Dario says. "Plus Santo. We are two."

"We have the high ground. And we have the element of surprise."

"We had the element of surprise," he corrects.

A red light blinks on the console near the glass. A silent alarm.

Below, the men in gray look up in unison. Twelve suppressors raise toward the gallery glass.

"Fuck," I hiss.

"Get back!" Dario roars.

He tackles me. His body hits mine with the force of a freight train, driving me into the hard floor just as the glass shatters.

It doesn't break like a window. It disintegrates under the concentrated fire of twelve submachine guns. The air fills with the screaming whine of ricochets and the dusting of safety glass.

We scramble backward, boots slipping on the debris. Bullets chew up the ceiling, raining concrete dust down on us.

"We're pinned!" I shout over the noise.

"We need cover!"

Dario grabs my vest and drags me behind a heavy steel pillar. We endure the storm. The sound is deafening—a continuous, ripping canvas of gunfire. They are suppressing us, keeping our heads down while a team moves to flank.

"They know we're here," Dario yells, checking his pistol. "They aren't shooting to scare. They're shooting to liquidate."

"We can't stay here. They'll come up the stairs."

"The stairs are a choke point." Dario slams a fresh magazine into his rifle. "But twelve against two in a hallway... that is just math. Eventually, the math wins."

I look around. The gallery is a dead end. One way in, one way out. And the Paladin team is already moving to block the exit.

I look at Dario. He is bleeding from a cut on his cheek where a shard of glass sliced him. He looks alive. Vibrant. The violence suits him better than the silence ever did.

"Do you trust me?" he asks.

"We are way past that question."

"The glass," he says, gesturing to the shattered window overlooking the warehouse floor. "It's a twenty-foot drop."

"Better than a bullet in a corner."

"I cover. You jump. You find cover behind the crates. Then you cover me."

"And if I break a leg?"

"Then I carry you out." A dark, reckless amusement lights his face. "Or we die together. Either way, we leave this room."

He doesn't wait for an answer. He rolls out from behind the pillar.

He fires. The boom of his unsuppressed rifle is a cannon shot in the enclosed space. He isn't spraying and praying. He is placing shots. One. Two. Three.

Below, a man screams.

"Go!" Dario shouts.

I sprint.

I run through the hail of glass and lead. I don't look at the muzzles tracking me. I look at the void where the window used to be.

I launch myself into the air.

For a second, I am weightless. The warehouse opens up around me, a vast cathedral of pain. I see the girls in the cages looking up, their faces masks of terror. I see El Santo retreating behind a wall of guards.

Then gravity claims me.

I hit a stack of wooden pallets. I roll, the impact jarring my teeth, my shoulder slamming into wood. I tumble to the concrete floor, gasping.

Pain flares in my hip, hot and sharp, but nothing is broken.

I scramble behind a forklift. I bring my rifle up.

"Dario!" I scream.

He is still up there, a dark silhouette against the gallery lights, firing down into the gray mass of the enemy. He is drawing their hate, making himself the target so I can breathe.

He vaults the ledge.

He drops like a stone, landing in a crouch ten feet to my left. He absorbs the impact with a grunt, rolls, and comes up shooting.

We are on the floor now. In the kill box.

Bullets spark off the forklift. The noise is incredible. The smell of cordite overpowers the frankincense.

"Flash out!" I yell, pulling the pin on a flashbang.

I hurl it over the forklift toward the advancing team.

BANG.

The white light blinds the world.

"Move up!" I order. "To the cages! We use the hostages as a shield! They won't fire on the merchandise!"

"Ruthless," Dario grunts, moving beside me. "I like it."

We advance. We move as a single organism, leapfrogging from cover to cover. I fire, he moves. He fires, I move. We drop two mercenaries in the open.

We reach the first row of cages.

The girls are screaming now. The conditioning has broken. The chaos has terrified them back into humanity.

"Get down!" I yell at them in Spanish. "*¡Al suelo!*"

They drop.

We slide behind a heavy steel workbench near the center of the room. We have a field of fire. We have cover.

But we are surrounded.

"Ammo check," Dario says. He is breathing hard, sweat dripping from his nose.

"Two mags left. Pistol is full."

"I have one mag."

He looks at the heavy door at the far end of the warehouse. More men are pouring in.

"This is it," he says. "The Alamo."

I look at him. There is blood on his face, dust in his hair, and a ferocity in his eyes that makes my heart hammer against my ribs.

"We buy them time," I say. "We make enough noise that someone has to notice."

"No one is coming, Merritt. We are the noise."

He reaches out and grabs my hand. His grip is crushing. It grounds me.

"If they take us," he says, his voice dropping so low only I can hear it over the gunfire. "Do not let them take you alive. You know what they do here."

I look at the cattle prod lying in the dust where El Santo dropped it. I look at the girls.

"I know."

I squeeze his hand back.

"Then let's make them pay for every inch."

A voice booms over the PA system. It isn't the synthesized prayer. It is human, cultured, and American.

Agent Gage. Mr. Ferri. This is unnecessary.

I freeze. I know that voice. I heard it at the gala. I heard it giving a toast to Julian's memory.

It's Councilman Reeves.

You have seen the operation. You understand the economics. We are simply fulfilling a supply chain demand. Throw out your weapons. There is a place for talent like yours in the organization.

I look at Dario. He bares his teeth in a wolfish grin.

"He thinks we are for sale," Dario says.

I stand up, using the workbench as a brace for my rifle.

"Hey Reeves!" I scream.

The firing stops. The silence stretches, taut and vibrating.

"My partner's name was Jack!" I yell. "And he wasn't for sale either!"

I aim for the speaker mounted on the wall. I fire.

The speaker explodes in a shower of sparks.

The answer is given.

The firing resumes, heavier than before. The air turns to lead. We huddle behind the steel, shoulder to shoulder, waiting for the end.

But then, a different sound cuts through the chaos.

A low, rhythmic *thump-thump-thump* that I feel in my chest before I hear it.

Dario looks up. "Do you hear that?"

The roof of the warehouse shakes. Dust rains down.

"Chopper," I say. "Reinforcements?"

"No," Dario says, his eyes narrowing. "That is a heavy lift rotor. That is..."

BOOM.

The skylight above the center of the warehouse explodes inward.

A massive crate on a parachute drops through the hole, slamming into the concrete floor between us and the Paladin team.

The crate bursts open.

It isn't supplies. It's guys.

Four men in mismatched armor, carrying AK-47s and machetes, roll out of the debris. They aren't Paladin. They aren't regular cartel.

They are wearing the colors of the *Diablos*—Dario's rival faction. The ones who wanted him dead.

"Your friends?" I ask, confused.

Dario stares at them. "No. Enemies."

The lead Diablo spots Dario. He spots the Paladin mercs. He grins.

"Hey, Ferri!" the man shouts. "Nobody kills you but us!"

The Diablos open fire on the Paladin team.

Chaos erupts. A three-way firefight. The enemy of my enemy has just crashed through the roof, not to save us, but to steal the kill.

"Unbelievable," I mutter.

Dario laughs. It is a harsh, barking sound.

"The ecosystem corrects itself," he says. He reloads his last magazine. "Now we have a distraction. Go for the controls. Release the locks on the cages."

"What about you?"

"I'm going to introduce El Santo to his maker."

He breaks cover, sprinting into the crossfire, a demon of vengeance let off the leash.

I turn toward the control panel on the far wall. The path is clear for three seconds.

I run.

I am not the Shield anymore. I am the Sword. And I am going to burn this temple to the ground.

CHAPTER ELEVEN

FATAL FUNNEL

The storm broke the moment we cleared the warehouse perimeter.

It wasn't a gradual buildup. It was a hammer drop. The sky, already bruised and heavy, tore open, unleashing a deluge that turned the dirt track into a river of mud. The wind howled off the Pacific, carrying the taste of salt and the distant, rhythmic *thump* of heavy machinery.

I slammed my shoulder against the corrugated metal of the maintenance shed we'd breached. My boots slipped on the wet concrete. My lungs burned, a raw fire in my chest that tasted of copper and cordite.

"Clear," I rasped, though the word was barely audible over the rain hammering the roof.

Dario kicked the door shut behind us. He threw the deadbolt, then jammed a steel chair under the handle. The barricade was symbolic at best. If Paladin or the Diablos wanted in, a piece of furniture wouldn't stop them. But it bought us seconds. And seconds were the only currency we had left.

He turned. In the gloom of the shed, lit only by the gray light filtering through the grime-streaked windows, he looked like a ruin. Blood dark and wet on the sleeve of his combat shirt. Dust from the explosion matted in his hair. But his eyes—black, flat, and terrifyingly calm—were fixed on me.

"Sit," he ordered.

I didn't argue. My legs felt like water. I slid down the wall until I hit the floor, my rifle clattering across my lap. The adrenaline dump was hitting me now, the chemical crash that leaves you shaking and cold.

Dario crossed the space between us in two strides. He dropped to one knee, ignoring the grime on the floor. His hands were on me instantly. Not asking. Taking inventory.

"Where?" he demanded.

"I'm fine. Just winded."

"Don't lie to me, Merritt."

His fingers probed my ribcage. I hissed, flinching away.

"Bruised," he diagnosed, his voice rough. "Maybe cracked. Your vest took the hit, but the energy has to go somewhere."

He moved to my arm. A jagged tear in the tactical fabric revealed a line of red seeping into the black material. A graze from a ricochet.

He reached into his med kit and ripped open a pack of clotting gauze.

"This will sting."

He pressed the gauze into the wound. The pain was sharp, electric, a white flash that cut through the exhaustion. I grit my teeth, locking a groan in my throat. I refused to make a sound. I was an agent of the United States government. I was a weapon. Weapons didn't whine.

Dario watched my face. A muscle feathered in his jaw.

"Breathe," he murmured. "You are holding it like a grenade."

"We need to move," I said, forcing the words out through clenched teeth. "The Diablos won't hold Paladin off forever. Once the mercenaries regroup, they'll sweep the island. We have maybe an hour."

"We have less. The storm is closing the extraction window." He taped the gauze down with quick, efficient movements. "But you cannot fight if you bleed out."

He finished the dressing. His hand didn't pull away. It lingered on my arm, his thumb resting against the pulse point of my wrist. His skin was rough, calloused, hot against the chill of the rain-soaked air.

The contact was heavy. It wasn't the touch of a medic anymore. It was the touch of a man claiming ownership of the damage.

My heart hammered against my ribs, a traitorous rhythm that had nothing to do with the pain. I looked at him. The distance between us was nonexistent. I could smell him—gun oil, sweat, the iron tang of blood, and the deep, underlying scent of the ocean.

"You move well," he said quietly. "For a Fed."

"I trained with the best."

"You fight like you have nothing to lose." His thumb stroked my skin, a slow, deliberate friction that sent a jolt straight to my core. "That makes you dangerous, *tesoro*. And reckless."

"Reckless got us out of that warehouse."

"Reckless got you thrown off a balcony." His eyes narrowed. "Next time, you wait for my signal."

"There won't be a next time if we don't finish this."

I pulled my arm back. The loss of his touch left a cold spot on my skin. I reached into my vest pouch and pulled out the satellite phone. It was heavy, rubberized, built to survive war zones.

"Who are you calling?" Dario asked. He stood up, towering over me, checking the load on his rifle.

"My handler. Miller. I need to update the threat assessment. If Paladin is operating a black site on foreign soil with government contracts, this goes beyond a drug bust. This is treason. We need a JSOC team. We need extraction for the girls."

Dario didn't laugh. He didn't scoff. He just looked at me with a profound, weary pity that made my stomach turn over.

"Make the call," he said. "But don't expect the cavalry."

I powered on the device. It searched for a signal, the bars blinking sluggishly. *Acquiring satellite...*

I stood up, wincing as my ribs protested. I walked to the window. The rain slashed against the glass, blurring the world outside into a smear of gray and green.

Signal Locked.

I dialed the emergency line. It rang once. Twice.

"Gage."

Miller's voice was clear, too clear. No static. He sounded like he was sitting in an office in D.C., sipping coffee while I stood in hell.

"Miller," I said. "We have a Situation critical. Mark the time. I am initiating a Code Black."

"Merritt?" His tone shifted. "Jesus, where have you been? We've been trying to ping your location for forty-eight hours. The Director is climbing the walls."

"Listen to me. The Baja intel was correct, but the scope is wrong. It's not just narcotics. It's human trafficking. Industrial scale. They're using the Vance shipping lanes."

"Okay," Miller said. "Slow down. Are you secure?"

"Negative. We are hostile. But listen—the security force isn't cartel. It's Paladin Global. I have visual confirmation on American PMCs running a conditioning facility. They are reprogramming children, Miller. They are scrubbing their minds."

Silence.

The line hummed with the dead space of a encrypted connection.

"Miller?"

"I hear you, Merritt." His voice was flat. Controlled. "Do you have the assets?"

"We have the girls. We're pinned down on the north side of the island. I need a QRF. I need chopper support. Get the Marines from the consulate. Get someone."

More silence. Then, a heavy sigh.

"Merritt, listen to me very carefully. You need to stand down."

The world stopped. The rain against the roof faded to a dull roar.

"Say again?"

"Stand down. Drop your weapons. Surrender to the Paladin containment team. They have been instructed to take you into custody without harm."

I gripped the phone so hard the plastic creaked.

"Custody? Miller, these men are skinning kids. They are monsters."

"They are contractors, Agent Gage. Operating under a classified DHS shield."

The blood drained from my face. My knees felt weak.

"You knew," I whispered. "You knew Paladin was here."

"The border crisis is... complex," Miller said. He sounded tired. He sounded like a man reading from a script. "We have overflow. We have thousands of unaccompanied minors. The system broke, Merritt. Paladin offered a solution. A private partnership to handle the processing and rehabilitation."

"Rehabilitation?" A laugh tore out of my throat, jagged and sharp. "Is that what they call it? They are torturing them. They are turning them into soldiers for the cartels."

"That is an operational anomaly. We are looking into it. But you—you are a rogue agent operating outside your jurisdiction with a known international fugitive. You are holding a match in a powder keg."

I looked at Dario. He was leaning against the peeling paint of the far wall, watching me. He didn't need to hear the other side of the conversation. He knew the song. He knew the lyrics. He had been singing them for years.

"Miller," I said, my voice shaking. "If you don't send help, I'm going to kill them. I'm going to kill every single one of them."

"If you fire another shot, Merritt, you are done. There is no coming back. You will be designated a domestic terrorist. We will hunt you. And we will not miss."

"Is that a threat?"

"It's a fact. Come in from the cold. Let us handle it."

"Handle it like you handled Jack?"

The name hung in the air. Jack. My partner. The man they said died in a random gang hit. The man whose skull was crushed because he found the shipping manifests.

"Jack didn't understand the big picture," Miller said softly. "Don't make his mistake."

I didn't say goodbye.

I didn't scream.

I lowered the phone from my ear. The connection was still live. I could hear Miller calling my name, tiny and tinny against the vastness of the betrayal.

Merritt? Agent Gage? Respond.

I looked at the device. It was a lifeline. It was a chain.

I walked to the door. I kicked the chair away and threw the bolt.

The wind hit me instantly, tearing at my clothes, soaking me to the bone in seconds. The ocean raged below the cliff, a black, churning cauldron of whitecaps and violence.

I stepped out into the rain. I raised my arm and hurled the phone.

It watched it arc through the grey sky, a small black geometric shape against the chaos of nature. It hit the water and vanished.

Gone.

The career. The pension. The badge. The belief that there was a line between the good guys and the bad guys, and that I stood on the right side of it.

It all sank into the Pacific.

I stood there for a moment, letting the rain wash the civilized world off my skin. I felt light. Terrifyingly light. The weight of the law was gone, and in its place was something colder, sharper.

I turned back to the shed.

Dario was standing in the doorway. He hadn't moved to stop me. He hadn't said a word. He just watched, a dark sentinel in the storm.

I walked back to him. I was dripping wet, shivering, my hair plastered to my skull.

"They aren't coming," I said.

"I know."

"They knew about Paladin. They signed the checks."

"The government is a business, Merritt. Morality is just marketing."

He reached out. He took my hand. His grip was warm, solid, the only real thing left in a world of smoke and mirrors. He pulled me inside, out of the wind.

He didn't let go of my hand. He pulled me closer until the toes of my boots touched his. He looked down at me, and for the first time, I saw something other than the predator. I saw the partner.

"Now you are free," he said.

"I have nothing."

"You have a rifle," he corrected. "And you have me."

He lifted a hand and brushed a wet strand of hair from my forehead. The gesture was shockingly intimate, a ghost of tenderness in the middle of a war zone.

"The Shield is broken," he whispered.

"Yes."

"Good." His eyes darkened, the black fire rekindling. "Shields are for defending. We are done defending."

He released me and walked to the crate where we had stashed the heavy ordnance. He picked up a claymore mine.

"The storm will ground their air support," he said, his voice shifting back to the tactical grind. "They are blind. They are deaf. And they are trapped on this rock with us."

I picked up my rifle. I checked the chamber. Brass gleamed in the darkness.

"They wanted a monster," I said.

I racked the slide. *Click-clack.*

"Let's show them what one looks like."

*

The tunnels beneath the compound were older than the Paladin tech. They were cartel tunnels—narrow, suffocating veins dug through the limestone by desperate men with pickaxes. They smelled of mold and old urine.

Dario took point. He moved with a crouched, predatory grace, the beam of his weapon light cutting a white cone through the darkness. The air was thick, suffocating. Every breath felt like inhaling wet wool.

We weren't running anymore. We were infiltrating.

"Schematics show the generator room is three hundred meters north," Dario whispered. "If we cut the power, we kill the mag-locks on the cages. The girls can run."

"And the guards?"

"They will be busy with us."

We reached a junction. A metal grate overhead filtered gray light and rain down onto the muddy floor. I paused, looking up. I could see boots moving across the grate. Gray digital camo.

Paladin.

They were right on top of us.

Dario signaled *halt*. He killed his light.

We stood in absolute darkness. I could hear his breathing—steady, slow. I could hear the rapid *thud-thud-thud* of my own heart.

Then, a sound echoed down the tunnel from behind us.

Splash.

It was faint. Careful. But unmistakable.

Someone was in the tunnel with us.

Dario spun around. He didn't speak. He pressed me against the damp limestone wall, covering my body with his. He drew his knife. The blade made no sound leaving the sheath.

We waited.

The footsteps got closer.

A beam of light swung around the corner, blindingly bright in the pitch black.

Dario moved.

He lunged out of the darkness, grabbing the wrist holding the light and twisting. A yelp of pain. The light clattered to the ground, spinning, casting wild shadows against the stone.

Dario slammed the intruder against the wall, the knife pressed to his throat.

"Wait!" the man choked out. "Don't kill me! Please!"

I grabbed the light and shone it on the man's face.

He was young. Skinny. Wearing a technician's jumpsuit with the Paladin logo. He wasn't a soldier. He was a kid with a laptop bag.

"Who are you?" I demanded, leveling my rifle at his chest.

"Simmons," he stammered, eyes wide with terror as he looked from Dario's knife to my muzzle. "I'm—I'm IT. I just handle the servers. I didn't sign up for this!"

Dario pressed the blade harder. A bead of blood welled up under the steel.

"You work for the butchers," Dario growled. "That makes you meat."

"No! I—I can help you!" Simmons scrambled, desperate. "I saw you on the feeds! I saw what you did in the warehouse. You're trying to stop El Santo, right?"

"We are going to kill him," Dario corrected.

"I can get you in," Simmons gasped. "The main door is biometric. You can't breach it. It's blast-proof. But I have an admin bypass."

I looked at Dario. He didn't lower the knife. He didn't trust easily. Neither did I. But we were out of options.

"Why help us?" I asked.

Simmons looked at me. He looked young enough to be in college. His hands were shaking.

"Because I saw the cages," he whispered. "I... I have a little sister. I can't do this anymore."

Dario stared at him for a long beat. Weighing the risk. Then, slowly, he pulled the knife back.

"If you are lying," Dario said, his voice a low rumble, "I will peel you apart."

"I'm not lying." Simmons rubbed his throat, swallowing hard. "But we have to hurry. They're flooding the lower levels. They're going to flush the tunnels with seawater to clear them out."

"Flooding?" I asked.

"The storm surge," Simmons said. "They opened the sea gates. The water is coming."

As if on cue, a low groan echoed through the tunnel. The sound of rushing water, distant but building.

"Move," Dario ordered.

He grabbed Simmons by the collar and shoved him forward.

We ran.

The tunnel floor was slick. The sound of the water grew louder, a roar chasing us through the dark. We splashed through puddles that were getting deeper by the second.

"Left!" Simmons shouted at the next junction. "The maintenance ladder!"

We scrambled up the rusted rungs just as a wall of black water surged past beneath us, filling the tunnel we had been standing in seconds ago. The spray hit my boots, cold and violent.

We climbed into a narrow service corridor. We were inside the main complex now. The air was colder here. Conditioned.

Simmons tapped a code into a keypad on a heavy steel door. *Green light.*

"This leads to the sub-basement," he whispered. "The boiler room."

Dario pushed past him, weapon raised. He cleared the room. It was empty, filled with the hum of massive machinery.

He turned to me. "We are in."

"Now the hard part," I said.

I looked at Simmons. "Where is the control room from here?"

"Two floors up. But the stairwell is guarded. They have a mounted gun."

Dario looked at the heavy steam pipes running up through the ceiling. He looked at the pressure valves.

"We don't need the stairs," Dario said. A cruel smile touched his lips. "We create a diversion."

He pointed to the main pressure valve for the heating system.

"If we blow that," he said, "steam vents through the entire ventilation system. It will blind the sensors. It will burn anyone in the corridors."

"It will cook the guards," I said.

Dario looked at me. "Yes."

I thought about Miller. I thought about the files he wanted to bury. I thought about the girls.

"Do it," I said.

Dario spun the valve. He rigged a breaching charge to the manifold.

"Fire in the hole," he whispered.

BOOM.

The explosion rocked the foundation. A scream of escaping steam shrieked through the building, a banshee wail that signaled the end of the polite world.

Alarms blared. Red lights flashed.

Dario looked at me through the haze. He held out his hand.

"Ready to burn it down?"

I took his hand. It was an anchor. It was a promise.

"Let's go."

We moved into the steam, ghosts in the machine, coming for the souls they tried to steal. The complications were over. The execution had begun.

CHAPTER TWELVE

A SIGNAL THROUGH THE STATIC

The heavy iron door of the supply bunker slammed shut, severing the scream of the steam vents. The silence that followed was sudden and absolute, ringing in my ears like the aftermath of an explosion.

Dario threw the bolt. The mechanism engaged with a definitive *thunk*.

We were sealed in.

The room was a concrete box, smelling of grease, oxidizing metal, and the damp, salt-heavy scent of the sea that clung to our clothes. A single caged bulb overhead flickered, casting a sickly yellow light that swung with the vibrations of the pounding storm outside.

I leaned back against the cold wall, sliding down until my boots hit the concrete. My lungs burned. Every breath felt like inhaling broken glass. The adrenaline that had carried me through the tunnels, past the guards, and into the boiler room was receding, leaving behind a hollow, shaking exhaustion.

Dario didn't sit. He paced.

He moved like a tiger in a cage—too big for the space, too full of kinetic energy to be contained. He checked the perimeter of the ten-by-ten room. He checked his sidearm. He checked the door he had just locked.

"They will need time to bypass the steam," he said, his voice a low rumble that vibrated in the small space. "The heat sensors are blinded. We have twenty minutes before they cut the vent flow and move in."

"Twenty minutes," I repeated.

It sounded like a lifetime. It sounded like nothing.

He turned to me.

The yellow light caught the sharp angles of his face, highlighting the smear of grease on his cheekbone and the dark, wet hair plastered to his forehead. He had stripped off his tactical vest in the tunnel, leaving only the black combat shirt.

It was soaked through. The fabric adhered to him, translucent in places, mapping the topography of a body built for violence.

I stopped breathing.

My gaze traveled over him, not as an agent assessing a threat, but as a woman starving for something solid. The shirt strained across the vast, hard expanse of his chest. His shoulders were broad enough to carry the weight of the sins he committed daily. But it was his arms that held me hostage. The sleeves were rolled up to his elbows, revealing forearms that were thick, roped with muscle, and mapped with veins that stood out like river systems under the skin.

They were scarred. Burn marks. Knife slashes. A history of survival written in raised white keloids against olive skin.

Those hands had snapped necks. Those hands had fired the shot
that saved my life in the warehouse. And ten minutes ago, those hands
had held mine with a tenderness that terrified me more than the gun.

A dark, heavy heat uncoiled in my stomach. It wasn't rational. We
were hunted. We were bleeding. Death was scratching at the door. But
the proximity to the end only made the biological imperative scream
louder. *Live. Feel. Burn.*

"Merritt."

He stopped pacing. He stood in the center of the room, looking
down at me. His eyes were black pits, devoid of light but full of gravity.

"You are staring."

"I'm looking at the only thing in this room that isn't terrifying," I
lied. He was terrifying. That was the point.

"We need to rest. Check your gear."

"Screw the gear."

I shoved off the wall. My legs trembled—not from fear, but from
the adrenaline crash leaving me hollow. I closed the distance between
us, boots colliding with his, and tilted my head back to meet the abyss
in his gaze.

"We have twenty minutes." My voice was steady, defying the tremor
in my hands. "Do not waste them counting bullets."

Dario went still. The air turned viscous, charged with the ozone
scent of violence and the musk of unwashed bodies.

"How do you want to spend them?" His voice dropped, a subter-
ranean rumble that vibrated through the floorboards.

I reached out. My hand, usually steady on a trigger, shook as I
pressed my palm flat against his chest. Through the blood-crusted
shirt, his heart hammered—a erratic, violent rhythm. A war drum
beating a retreat for sanity.

"Remind me I'm flesh," I whispered. "Prove I'm not just a weapon you point at the enemy."

He trapped my hand under his. His palm was calloused sandpaper, scorching hot. He didn't offer comfort; he crushed my fingers against his pectoral muscle, grinding bone against bone.

"You are flesh. You are blood. You are a fucking liability."

"Then punish me."

His pupils blew wide, swallowing the iris until his eyes were entirely black. He saw the rot in me, the reckless, suicidal need to be unmade.

"Merritt. If I start..."

"Do I look like I'm retreating?"

A sound tore from his throat—part snarl, part desperate groan. His restraint snapped like a dry twig.

He seized my waist, iron fingers digging into the soft flesh of my sides, and hurled me backward. My back slammed into the steel shelving unit. Cans of gun oil clattered to the floor, the stench of petroleum mixing with the copper tang of blood.

I didn't flinch. I wrapped my legs around him, dragging his hips into the cradle of mine.

His mouth crushed mine. A collision of teeth and tongue. He tasted of rust and salt and dominance. He plundered my mouth, biting my lower lip hard enough to split the skin, drinking the bead of blood that welled up.

He ripped his mouth away, his forehead knocking against mine hard enough to bruise.

"The Shield," he growled, his grip on my thighs tightening to painful pressure points. "You think you have to be hard. Unbreaking."

"I have to survive."

"Not with me. With me, you break."

He released my legs. My boots hit the concrete, but I swayed, drunk on his proximity.

"Turn around."

The command cracked like a pistol shot.

My training screamed. *Never give up your back. Maintain the perimeter.* But the dark, twisting thing in my gut—the bitch who craved to be possessed—silenced the agent.

I turned. I gripped the cold steel shelf, knuckles bleaching white.

"Hands behind your back."

I hesitated on the precipice.

"Now, Merritt."

I surrendered. I swept my hands back.

He caught my wrists in one large hand. I heard the rustle of gear, then the rough bite of paracord. He wound it tight, ruthless loops cutting into my skin, binding my wrists together. Not safe. Not gentle. It was tight enough to chafe, tight enough to render me utterly at his mercy.

Control evaporated. The Shield shattered into dust.

"Dario..." Panic fluttered in my throat, a frantic bird trapped in a cage.

"I have you." His breath was a furnace against the nape of my neck, sending shivers cascading down my spine. "Stop thinking. Stop leading. Just feel."

He swept my hair aside, exposing the pale, vulnerable column of my neck. He bit down on the pulse point, hard, claiming me.

"You belong to me," he snarled against my skin. "In the dark. In the blood. Mine."

His hands stormed the front of my pants. Belt unbuckled. Zipper ripped down. He shoved the tactical fabric past my hips, his rough palms scraping against my waist, leaving trails of fire.

The bunker air bit at my exposed skin, freezing cold, but where his body pressed against my back, I was an incinerator.

He ground his hips against my ass. He was hard, a rigid serenity pressing through his trousers.

"Please," I whimpered. The word tasted like ash. I needed him to ruin me.

"Patience."

He slid a hand between my thighs.

My head thumped forward against the steel shelf. He found my slick, weeping heat instantly. He groaned, the vibration travelling through his chest into my spine.

"So fucking wet," he murmured, fingers sliding through the slime. "Leaking for me."

"Yes. Always."

He didn't prep me. He didn't care about comfort. I heard his zipper rasp, the sound of a guillotine blade dropping.

The blunt head of his cock pressed against my entrance.

I tensed. He was too thick, impossible.

"Relax." He grabbed my hip, fingers bruising, anchoring me. "Take it, Merritt. Take every inch."

I exhaled, forcing my walls to drop.

He drove inside.

It was a violation and a homecoming. He split me open, stretching me beyond capacity, invading the deepest, darkest corners of my anatomy. It felt like he was rearranging my organs, carving his name into my cervix.

I screamed, a raw, ragged sound that bounced off the concrete.

He stopped, buried to the hilt, sheathed fully in my tight, wet heat.

We froze in the fusion. Predator and prey. The line between where the tactical agent ended and the woman began dissolved in a haze of endorphins.

"Look at me."

He wrenched my shoulder back. I turned my head, meeting his gaze.

His face was a mask of agony and ecstasy. Eyes wide, unguarded, black holes promising oblivion.

"Feel that?" he rasped.

"Yes."

"That is real. The rest is just noise."

He began to piston without mercy.

He pulled back and slammed home, the slap of his hips against my ass echoing in the small room. The friction was blinding, a white-hot current electrifying my nerves.

My bound hands strained against the cord. I needed to claw him. I needed to fight back. But I was helpless, pinned by his weight and his cock, forced to just *take*.

"Dario," I sobbed. The pressure built in my belly, a tidal wave receding before the strike.

"I'm here," he grunted, pace increasing to a punishing rhythm. "Taking what's mine."

He reached around, splaying a large hand over my stomach, pressing me back against his thrusts. His thumb dug down, finding the bundle of nerves above my clit, adding a sharp, electric spike to the blunt trauma of his penetration.

My knees buckled. Only his grip kept me upright.

"Don't close your eyes," he ordered. "Watch me break you."

I stared at the sweat dripping from his temple.

The wave crested.

"Dario!"

I shattered.

My body clamped down on his steel length, milking him, convulsing in violent, spasmodic contractions. My scream tore my throat raw. Pleasure, hot and absolute, scoured away the fear, the mission, the memory of the death waiting outside.

He roared my name.

He hammered into me one last time, bottoming out, and froze. His muscles turned to stone. He poured himself into me, thick, hot jets of seed flooding my womb, marking me inside and out.

We stayed locked together, breathing in ragged gasps, the smell of sex and musk overpowering the metallic tang of the room.

Slowly, Dario withdrew.

My legs gave out.

He caught me before I hit the floor. He spun me around, hauling me against his chest. He didn't untie me. He held me captive in his arms, face buried in the crook of my neck, inhaling the scent of my sweat.

"I have you," he whispered. "I have you."

I slumped against him, the chaotic thrum of his heart slowing against my ear. I felt raw. Scraped clean. Owned.

He reached behind me, fingers working the knot. The paracord fell away.

I brought my hands forward, rubbing the angry red welts on my wrists. A visible claim. A brand.

Dario adjusted his clothes. He picked up his vest from the floor. He didn't look ashamed. He didn't look away. He looked restored.

He walked over to me, grabbed my chin, and tilted my face up. He examined me with that terrifying intensity.

"Better?" he asked. The same question from the server room.

"Different," I said.

"Good."

He kissed my forehead. A benediction.

Then he turned to the door. He picked up his rifle and racked the slide. The sound was a harsh return to reality.

"Ten minutes left," he said. "We need to move before they cut the steam."

I pulled my pants up. I fastened my belt. I picked up my weapon. The weight of it felt different now. Lighter. Or maybe I was just stronger.

I wasn't just fighting for the mission anymore. I wasn't fighting for the badge.

I looked at Dario's broad back as he checked the peephole.

I was fighting for him. And God help anyone who tried to take him from me.

"Ready?" he asked, glancing back.

I stepped up beside him. The Shield was gone. The woman was awake.

"Open the door."

CHAPTER THIRTEEN

SURGICAL ENTRY

The cold metal of the grappling hook bites into my palm, grounding me, even as my pulse tries to hammer its way out of my throat. It's a rhythmic, sickening thud—*run, run, run*. My survival instinct screams that the steam-choked shadows ahead are teeth, waiting to snap shut the moment I cross the threshold. I can feel the phantom weight of failure pressing against my lungs, a suffocating premonition of capture, of silence, of the end. I am too small for this fight, too fragile for the monsters lurking behind those reinforced walls.

But beneath the terror, there is the hunger.

It is a dark, molten heat in my belly that burns hotter than the fear. I don't just want the truth buried in that vault; I *need* it like oxygen. I need to see their empire crumble, and I crave the terrifying ecstasy of being the one to swing the hammer. This desire to break them is a narcotic, sweet and heavy in my blood. It steadies my trembling fingers. It sharpens the blurred edges of my panic into a weapon. One breath. Just one breath to bridge the gap between the girl who survived and the ghost I have to become.

"Merritt."

Dario's voice is a vibration against my spine before it registers as sound. He stands behind me in the service shaft, his chest a solid wall of heat against my back. The steam from the blown manifold hisses around us, a white curtain reducing the world to three feet of visibility.

"I'm ready," I say. My voice sounds strange to my own ears—scraped raw, stripped of the bureaucratic polish I wore for fifteen years.

"The sensor is blind," he murmurs, checking the load on the grappling line. "But the men are not. Up top, we are in the hive. No talking. Only killing."

He looks at me. The black fire in his eyes hasn't dimmed since the bunker. If anything, the violence has fed it. He reaches out, his thumb tracing the line of my jaw, a rough caress that feels like a claim of ownership.

"Stay on my six. Do not engage unless you have the kill."

"I know the drill, Dario."

"Good."

He throws the hook.

It soars upward through the haze, clattering against the metal grating of the ventilation intake three floors up. He gives it a tug. It holds.

He goes first. He ascends the rope with effortless, terrifying strength, his boots finding purchase on the slick concrete walls. I follow. My muscles protest—the bruises from the warehouse, the strain of the sex, the exhaustion—but the pain is distant. I am running on pure chemical drive now.

We reach the grate. Dario pulls a multitool from his vest. *Click. Snap.* The screws give way.

He pushes the grate up and slides into the crawlspace. I pull myself up after him.

The air here is different. The smell of the boiler room—grease and ozone—is gone. It is replaced by something sterile. Antiseptic. Underneath that, the faint, copper tang of old blood.

We crawl. The metal ductwork groans softly under our weight. Through the slats of the vents, I see flashes of the facility below. White floors. Men in lab coats moving with clipboards. Armed guards in Paladin gray standing at intersections.

Dario stops. He signals *halt*.

He points through a vent directly beneath us.

I look down.

My stomach turns over.

It isn't a lab. It's a dormitory. But there are no beds. Just rows of sleeping mats on a cold tile floor. And on the mats, boys. Dozens of them. They range from six years old to maybe twelve. They are sitting cross-legged, facing a large screen on the wall. They are perfectly still. Unnaturally still.

The screen flashes images. Fast. Violent. A man holding a gun. A burning church. A severed hand.

Audio plays over the room, a low, rhythmic chanting in Spanish.

La sangre limpia. El dolor salva. Obediencia es vida. (Blood cleanses. Pain saves. Obedience is life.)

"Conditioning," I whisper. The word tastes like bile.

Dario's hand tightens on his rifle until his knuckles bleach white. He knows this script. He lived a version of it in the streets of Naples, but this... this is industrial. This is a factory line for sociopaths.

"They are breaking them," he says, his voice a low grind of gravel. "Stripping the empathy out to make perfect soldiers."

He moves to the next vent section. He kicks it out.

"We go down," he says.

"Dario, the guards—"

"Quiet."

He drops.

He lands in the center of the aisle between the mats. The boys don't scream. They don't run. They just turn their heads, slowly, in unison. Their eyes are empty. Dead glass.

Two guards at the far door spin around, raising their carbines.

Dario is faster.

He doesn't use his rifle. He draws the silenced USP from his hip. *Phut-phut.*

The first guard drops, a dark hole in his forehead.

The second guard fumbles with his radio. Dario closes the distance in three strides. He grabs the man's barrel, twists it aside, and drives a combat knife into the man's throat.

The guard gurgles, sliding down the wall.

I drop down behind Dario, my rifle up, scanning the corners.

"Clear," I hiss.

Dario wipes the blade on the guard's uniform. He turns to the boys.

"Listen to me!" he barks in Spanish. "You are leaving. Now."

They don't move. They stare at him like he is part of the test.

One of the older boys, maybe ten, stands up. He walks toward Dario. He holds a sharpened piece of plastic—a toothbrush handle filed to a needle point.

"The Saint says intruders are tests," the boy recites tonelessly. "We must pass the test."

I lower my weapon. "Kid, no. We're here to help."

The boy lunges.

It's clumsy, slow. Dario catches the boy's wrist effortlessly. He twists, forcing the shiv from the kid's hand. He doesn't break the arm. He doesn't strike. He kneels, bringing his face level with the child.

"The Saint is a liar," Dario says softly. "Look at me."

The boy trembles. The programming wars with the instinct.

"The Saint eats well while you starve," Dario says. "He sleeps in silk while you sleep on stone. Is that a god? or is that a parasite?"

The boy blinks. Confusion cracks the mask.

"Go to the boiler room," Dario orders, pointing to the vent we came from. "Climb the rope. Wait in the dark. If you see men in gray, hide. If you see me, come out."

The boy looks at the rope. He looks at the other children.

"Run," Dario commands. The voice of a Don. Absolute.

The boy runs. The others follow, a silent tide of small, broken ghosts scrambling for the shadows.

"We can't save them all," I say, my throat tight. "Not if we don't kill the head."

"We move."

We exit the dormitory into the main corridor. The alarms haven't tripped yet—the steam in the lower levels is still causing chaos on the boards. But we are running out of time.

"The girls," I say. "Intel said Sector 4."

"This way."

We move tactically. Leapfrogging. I cover the high angles; he checks the corners. We flow like water.

We round a corner and run straight into a patrol. Three Paladin contractors.

No time for silencers.

"Contact front!" I yell.

I drop to a knee and fire. My rifle bucks against my shoulder. The lead man takes two rounds to the chest plate, staggers, and goes down.

Dario takes the left. He double-taps the second man.

The third man dives for cover behind a medical cart, spraying blind fire down the hall. Bullets spark off the wall inches from my head. Concrete dust stings my eyes.

"Suppressing!" I shout, pouring fire into the cart. Bottles shatter. Fluids explode.

Dario flanks. He moves with a terrifying, predatory speed, vaulting a gurney and landing beside the man.

The struggle is brief. Brutal. A sickening crack of bone.

Silence returns.

Dario stands up. He is breathing hard, a sheen of sweat on his face. He looks at me.

"Ammo check."

"Half mag."

He nods. He walks over to me. He doesn't stop at a tactical distance. He steps into my space, grabbing the back of my neck, pulling my forehead against his.

"You hesitated," he says.

"What?"

"The first shot. You aimed for the center mass. The vest caught it. Next time, take the head."

"I took the shot I had."

"Take the shot that kills," he growls. "Mercy is a luxury we left in the bunker."

His gaze drops to my mouth. For a second, the war recedes. The memory of his hands on me, inside me, floods my system. The heat flares again, sharp and insistent.

"Are we arguing tactics?" I whisper.

"I am sharpening my weapon." He kisses me hard, a bruise of a kiss that tastes of violence. "Stay sharp, *tesoro*. The hard part begins now."

He pulls away and kicks open the double doors marked *SECTOR 4 - RESTRICTED*.

We step through.

And stop.

This isn't a lab. It's a church.

The walls are draped in red velvet. Heavy, gold candelabras burn with thick wax candles, casting dancing shadows against the ceiling. The smell of frankincense is choking.

But in the center of the 'nave', there are no pews.

There are cages.

Chrome steel cages, suspended from the ceiling by chains. Inside each one is a girl. They are dressed in white communion dresses. Some are sleeping. Some are weeping silently.

And at the altar, standing with his back to us, is a man in a white linen suit.

El Santo.

He turns slowly. He doesn't look surprised. He looks delighted.

He holds a remote trigger in one hand and a microphone in the other.

"Welcome, pilgrims," his voice booms through the space, smooth and cultured. "I was wondering when the sinners would arrive to confess."

I raise my rifle. The dot of my optic settles between his eyes.

"Drop it!" I scream. "Federal Agent! Drop the remote!"

El Santo smiles. It is a terrible, beatific expression.

"You misunderstand the architecture, Agent Gage," he says. He raises the remote. "This isn't a weapon. It's a release valve."

He points to the cages.

"The floor beneath the penitents acts as a drain," he explains calmly. "But it also opens directly into the sea caves below. One press, and the floor drops out. They fall two hundred feet into the crushing dark."

My finger freezes on the trigger.

"You shoot me, my thumb slips," he says. "Gravity does the rest."

Dario steps forward. He lowers his weapon, but his body is coiled tight, a spring ready to snap.

"You like games, Santo?" Dario asks. His voice is conversational. Chilling.

"Mr. Ferri." El Santo nods. "I admire your resilience. Most men would have drowned by now."

"I don't drown," Dario says. He takes another step. "I burn."

"Stay back!" El Santo's thumb hovers over the button.

"You have a Deadman's switch," Dario observes. "Clever. But you are a businessman. You deal in product. Dropping the inventory is bad for margins."

"These aren't product anymore," El Santo says, his eyes gleaming with zealotry. "They are martyrs. If I cannot purify them, I will send them to God."

"Merritt," Dario says quietly. He doesn't look at me.

"I'm here."

"On my signal."

"What signal?"

"The one where I give you a clear shot."

Dario drops his rifle. It clatters loudly on the marble floor. He holds up his empty hands.

"Trade," Dario says.

El Santo cocks his head. "Trade?"

"Me for them." Dario opens his arms. "You want the King of the West Coast? You want the man who defied the Families? I am worth more than a dozen girls. You can break me. Imagine the prestige. Breaking Dario Ferri."

El Santo licks his lips. The ego hook sinks in.

"Walk to the altar," El Santo commands. "Hands where I can see them."

Dario walks.

Every step is a hammer blow to my chest. He is walking into the kill zone. He is offering himself up to the butcher.

Don't do it, I scream internally. *Don't you dare leave me here alone.*

But I know why he is doing it. He is closing the distance. He is buying me the angle.

Dario reaches the steps of the altar. He kneels.

El Santo steps closer, the remote still clutched tight, but his focus has shifted. He pulls a pistol from his waistband and presses it to Dario's forehead.

"Confess," El Santo whispers. "Confess your sins."

Dario looks up. He looks past the gun. He looks past the man. He looks at me.

And he winks.

"My sin," Dario says, his voice ringing through the silent church, "is that I didn't bring enough bullets."

He moves.

Not away from the gun. *Into* it.

He grabs the barrel of El Santo's pistol and jerks it down just as it fires. The bullet shatters a tile by his knee.

At the same time, he drives his shoulder into El Santo's gut, tackling him backward onto the altar.

The remote flies out of El Santo's hand. It skitters across the marble floor, spinning toward the edge of the platform.

"Merritt!" Dario roars.

I am already moving.

I sprint toward the remote. I have to get there before it stops sliding. Before it hits the wall and triggers the release.

A side door bursts open. Paladin guards spill out.

I don't stop. I fire from the hip—*bang, bang, bang*—suppressing them while I dive.

I hit the floor hard, sliding on the polished stone. My hand slaps down on the remote just as it teeters on the edge of the stair.

I clutch it to my chest, gasping.

I look up.

Dario and El Santo are a tangle of limbs on the altar. El Santo has a knife now. He slashes Dario's arm—a spray of bright red.

Dario doesn't flinch. He headbutts El Santo, a sickening *thud* of bone on bone. He grabs the man's hair and slams his face into the marble surface of the altar. Once. Twice.

The Paladin guards are advancing on me. I roll onto my back, bringing my rifle up.

Click.

Empty.

I draw my pistol.

"Dario! We have company!"

Dario looks up from his work. El Santo is unconscious, bleeding heavily.

Dario grabs El Santo's body and hauls him up as a human shield.

"Let them come!" he bellows, his face a mask of blood and fury.

He drags the limp body of the cult leader toward the control panel on the wall.

"Cover me!"

I fire until my slide locks back.

"Out!" I yell. "I'm dry!"

Dario reaches the panel. He punches the emergency release.

CLANG.

The cages above us shudder. The chains begin to lower.

"The disconnect is manual!" Dario shouts over the gunfire. "I have to hold the lever!"

"Hold it!"

I scramble behind a heavy stone pillar. I reload my pistol with shaking hands. I have one magazine left.

I look at Dario. He is exposed. He is holding the lever down with one hand, firing El Santo's pistol with the other. He is the only thing standing between the girls and the drop.

He catches my eye.

"Get them out!" he orders. "Get them to the boat!"

"I am not leaving you!"

"You are the Shield!" he screams. "Do your job!"

The cages hit the floor. The doors spring open.

The girls spill out, terrified, weeping.

I look at them. I look at Dario.

My heart rips in half.

"Go!" he roars.

I turn to the girls. "Move! Into the vents! Go!"

I herd them toward the extraction point. I look back one last time.

Dario is laughing. He is bleeding from three different wounds, surrounded by enemies, standing on an altar of madness. And he is laughing.

He is the Sword. And he is sharper than he has ever been.

I push the last girl into the duct. I climb in after her.

And I pray that the Sword doesn't break before I can come back for him.

CHAPTER FOURTEEN

THE ROOT AND THE ROT

The heavy oak door of the sacristy splintered under the impact of a boot, but the deadbolt held.

I didn't flinch. I didn't look at the door. I shoved the heavy mahogany desk across the marble floor, the legs screeching a protest that echoed through the vaulted ceiling. I slammed it against the door, adding three hundred pounds of solid wood to the barrier.

Thud.

Another blow from the outside. The wood groaned, but the barricade held.

They were screaming in Spanish on the other side. Threats. Orders. The panicked coordination of men who had lost their god and were now facing the devil.

I turned my back on them.

The room was silent, insulated from the chaos of the main church by two feet of stone. It smelled of beeswax, stale incense, and the copper tang of my own blood.

I looked down at my arm. The cut from El Santo's knife was deep, a dark red mouth grinning on my forearm. The blood dripped onto the pristine white Persian rug. *Drip. Drip.*

I didn't bind it. The pain was useful. It was a tether. It kept the rage focused, distilled into a cold, hard point.

Merritt was gone.

The thought hit me harder than the knife. I had sent her away. I had watched the vent swallow her, taking the only source of heat in this frozen hell with it.

I shouldn't have let her go.

The instinct to chase her, to drag her back and lock her down where I could see her, was a physical ache in my chest. It wasn't rational. It wasn't tactical. It was a hunger. A dark, starving thing that had woken up the moment I saw her breach that stash house in Baja.

She was the Shield. She was duty and law and rigid lines. And I wanted to be the one to shatter her, just to see how she put herself back together.

But she had to live. That was the bargain. I stayed. She ran.

Thud.

The door hinges whined.

"Open it, or we burn it down!" a voice shouted from the nave.

"Try it!" I roared back. "I'm sitting on the gas main!"

A lie. But fear was a better lock than steel. The shouting stopped. They were regrouping.

I had five minutes. Maybe ten.

I scanned the room.

It was a blasphemy of comfort. While the children slept on cold tiles, El Santo lived here. Silk tapestries covered the stone walls. A king-sized bed with velvet sheets dominated the corner. A bar cart stocked with rare tequilas sat under a crucifix made of platinum.

Hypocrisy. It was the only religion these animals truly practiced.

I moved to the wall behind the desk. A large oil painting of the Virgin Mary hung there. Her eyes were sorrowful, looking down at the sins of the room.

I gripped the gilded frame and ripped it off the wall.

Behind it, a wall safe. Digital keypad. Biometric scanner.

I didn't have the code. I didn't have El Santo's finger—I had left him bleeding on the altar.

But I had C4.

I reached into my pouch. A small block of plastic explosive, the size of a deck of cards. Enough to breach the hinge, not enough to collapse the wall. I pressed it into the seam of the safe door. I inserted the detonator.

I dragged a heavy wingback chair over and flipped it, crouching behind the upholstery.

"Fire in the hole."

I triggered the charge.

CRACK.

The room shook. Dust billowed from the wall. The heavy steel door of the safe clanged onto the floor, smoking.

I stood up, dusting off the debris. I walked to the hole in the wall.

Inside, there were no stacks of cash. No gold bars. El Santo knew better than to keep his wealth liquid where his lieutenants could steal it.

There was only a single, ruggedized hard drive and a leather-bound ledger.

I pulled them out.

I carried them to the small table by the liquor cart. I poured a glass of tequila, downed it in one swallow, and opened the ledger.

It wasn't an account of drug shipments. It wasn't a roster of soldiers.

It was a catalog.

*Subject 402. Male. Age 8. Origin: San Diego.

Destination: Riyadh.

Price: $150,000.*

*Subject 403. Female. Age 12. Origin: Los Angeles.

Destination: Private Estate, Seattle.

Price: $220,000.*

My hand tightened on the leather until the binding creaked.

They weren't just conditioning soldiers. They were filling orders. Custom requests for human misery.

I turned the page.

The next section wasn't sales. It was "Logistics and Acquisitions."

I scanned the columns. Dates. Transport routes. Border checkpoints that were miraculously unstaffed at specific times.

And the contacts.

My eyes snagged on a name. I stopped breathing.

The name appeared over and over. Authorizing the transport trucks. Signing off on the "agricultural" cargo inspections. Providing the encrypted comms gear for the island.

Julian Vance.

I stared at the name. The ink was black, definitive.

Julian Vance. The politician. The "Man of the People." The grieving brother-in-law who had stood by Merritt's side at the funeral, holding her hand while they lowered Jack into the ground.

Merritt spoke of him with a reverence she reserved for the dead. He was family. He was the one clean thing left in her life, the civilian who didn't know the war but supported the warrior.

I turned to the hard drive. I needed to know the depth of the rot.

There was a laptop on the side table. I booted it up, connected the drive. No password on the drive itself—arrogance again. They assumed no one would ever get this far.

I opened the folder marked *PARTNERS*.

Photos.

Grainy surveillance shots of meetings.

There was Julian Vance, shaking hands with El Santo on a yacht. Julian Vance, accepting a briefcase in a parking garage.

And then, a video file. Dated three years ago.

I clicked it.

The video was shaky, handheld. It showed a warehouse. Shipping containers.

Julian was there. He was younger, sweating, looking nervous. He was talking to a man in a cartel tactical vest.

"The route is clear," Julian was saying, his voice tinny through the speakers. "My office re-routed the patrol sectors. You have a two-hour window."

"And the cargo?" the cartel man asked.

"The kids are in the back," Julian said. He didn't look sick. He didn't look reluctant. He looked impatient. "Just get them out of my district before the election cycle starts. I can't have missing person reports spiking while I'm polling."

The video ended.

I sat back. The silence in the room was absolute, heavier than the stone walls.

This wasn't just corruption. This was a demolition of Merritt's reality.

She believed the system was broken but fixable. She believed that good men died trying to hold the line. She believed Jack died a hero, and Julian was the mourning survivor.

But Julian was the pipeline.

And Jack?

I clicked the next file. *INCIDENT REPORT: AGENT GAGE / AGENT REYNOLDS.*

A scanned email. From Julian Vance to El Santo.

Subject: Loose Ends.

Jack is asking too many questions. He found the discrepancies in the border logs. He knows about the trucks. He's going to bring it to Merritt. If she sees it, she won't stop. She's a dog with a bone.

Fix it. Make it look like a gang hit. And make sure Merritt finds the body. The trauma will distract her. She'll chase ghosts instead of the logistics.

I closed the laptop.

A cold, dark laughter bubbled up in my throat. It wasn't funny. It was horrific.

Jack Reynolds wasn't killed by the cartel. He was killed by his brother-in-law's ambition. He was executed because he got too close to the family business.

And Merritt? They had played her. For three years, they had used her grief as a blindfold. They pointed her at stash houses and low-level dealers, letting her vent her rage on the symptoms while the disease slept in her guest room.

She hunted monsters in the dark, never realizing the worst one was sitting at her Sunday dinner table.

My fist slammed into the table. The wood cracked. The empty tequila glass shattered, biting into my skin.

I didn't care.

I thought of her face in the bunker. The raw, open trust in her eyes when she let me bind her. The way she whispered *I have nothing* when she threw her phone into the sea.

She was wrong. She had less than nothing. She had a lie.

If she saw this... if she knew that the man she protected, the man she loved as family, was the architect of this hell...

It would kill her. The bullet wouldn't do it. The betrayal would. It would snap that steel spine of hers.

I looked at the drive.

I could destroy it. I could burn the ledger. I could kill Julian myself, bury him in the desert, and let her keep her illusion. Let her mourn a good man instead of discovering a monster.

It would be a mercy.

But mercy was for the weak. And Merritt Gage was not weak.

I stood up. I shoved the drive into my tactical vest, right against my heart. I tucked the ledger into my belt.

She deserved the truth. Even if it cut her throat.

Because she was mine. And I didn't share her with anyone, not even a ghost.

Thud. CRACK.

The barricade gave way. The desk slid across the floor as the door burst open.

Three Paladin guards filled the doorway, rifles raised.

"Drop it!" the point man screamed. "Hands!"

I looked at them.

I didn't see threats. I saw obstacles. I saw dead men walking who were standing between me and the woman I needed to save from herself.

I picked up my rifle from the table.

"You're late," I said.

The point man hesitated. He saw the blood on my arm. He saw the shattered glass. But mostly, he saw the look in my eyes.

He realized, too late, that they hadn't trapped me. They had just locked themselves in with the butcher.

"Contact!" he yelled.

I moved.

There was no cover. I didn't need it. I walked toward them, firing.

Bang. Bang. Bang.

Control. Rhythm. Violence.

The first man dropped, his throat opened. The second took a round to the knee and one to the chest.

The third man scrambled back, his nerve breaking. He fired blindly, the rounds chipping the stone around my head.

I didn't break stride. I stepped over the bodies. I raised the rifle.

Bang.

Silence returned.

I walked out of the sacristy, stepping into the nave. The air was thick with smoke. The cages lay on the floor like the ribs of a dead whale.

Sirens wailed in the distance. Mexican Marines. Or maybe more cartel reinforcements.

It didn't matter.

I touched the drive in my vest.

The war wasn't on this island anymore. The war was in California.

I keyed my radio.

"Merritt."

Static.

"Merritt, do you copy?"

Nothing.

"Frenzy, this is Ferri. Report."

A crackle. Then, her voice. Breathless. Wet. Alive.

"I hear you. We're at the boat. The kids are loaded. Where are you?"

Her voice was a lifeline. It pulled me out of the dark.

"I'm coming out," I said. "Start the engines."

"Dario... are you clear?"

I looked at the carnage around me. I looked at the blood on my hands.

"No," I said, walking toward the exit, toward the storm, toward her. "I'm just getting started."

I ejected the magazine and slammed a fresh one home.

Click-clack.

Julian Vance wanted a monster?

I was bringing him one.

*

The extraction was a blur of salt spray and diesel fumes.

The boat cut through the waves, a black wedge driving north. The storm was breaking, leaving behind a sky the color of a fresh bruise.

I stood at the stern, watching the island shrink into the horizon. A pillar of black smoke rose from the compound—my parting gift to the generator room.

Merritt stood beside me. She was wrapped in a thermal blanket, her hair wild, her face streaked with grime. She was watching the children huddled in the cabin.

She looked exhausted. Shattered. But her eyes were clear.

"We did it," she whispered. "We got them out."

She turned to me. She didn't ask about the blood on my arm. She just reached out and took my hand. Her fingers were cold.

"Thank you," she said. "For the distraction. For holding the line."

She squeezed my hand. A gesture of partnership. Of trust.

"We hurt them today, Dario. We really hurt them."

I looked down at her.

She looked so proud. So vindicated. She thought she had struck a blow for the righteous.

I felt the hard drive pressing against my ribs. The weight of it was suffocating.

"Merritt," I said. My voice was rougher than I intended.

"What?" She looked up, sensing the shift in my mood.

I wanted to tell her. I wanted to pull the drive out and end it right there. Rip the band-aid off.

But not here. Not with the children watching. Not while she was still shaking from the adrenaline.

I pulled her closer, wrapping my arm around her shoulders. I pulled her into the hard wall of my chest, burying my face in her wet, tangled hair.

"We aren't done," I murmured against her scalp.

"I know," she said, leaning into me. "But we won the battle."

"The war is different," I said.

I looked out at the ocean. The water was black, deep, and full of things that compel you to drown.

I held her tighter. I held her like I was trying to keep her from falling apart. Because I knew, as soon as we hit the shore, I was going to have to break her heart to save her life.

"Rest," I ordered. "I have the watch."

She nodded against my chest. Her breathing slowed. She trusted me to watch the horizon.

She didn't know the threat was already on the boat.

I stared north, toward the lights of California. Toward Julian.

I am coming for you, I thought, the promise cold and absolute. *And I am going to burn your world down with the truth.*

CHAPTER FIFTEEN

THE SWORD WITH NO SHEATH

The wood splintered under the impact of a heavy boot—a sound like a cracking spine—but I couldn't look away from her. Not for a second.

Merritt sat slumped against the industrial radiator, dust motes dancing in the harsh halo of the emergency light catching her hair. A smear of blood marked her cheek, bright and offensive against the pallor of her skin. The urge to wipe it away, to burn the world down for daring to make her bleed, rose in my chest like bile.

My hands shook. Not from the fear of the Paladin death squad stacking up in the hallway, but from the proximity of her mortality. She was the only thing that made this rot-filled world quiet. If they took her, the noise would come back. If they touched her, I would unravel. I was nothing but a violent ghost without her gravity holding me to the floor.

I gripped the pistol until my knuckles bleached white, the polymer grip biting into my palm. It was a grounding pain. I counted the heartbeats pulsing in the hollow of her throat. One. Two. Three. Each one a universe I had to defend.

The lock gave a final, metallic shriek.

"They're through," Merritt said. Her voice was rough, scraped raw by smoke and screaming, but it didn't tremble.

"Let them come." I racked the slide. "I still have ammunition."

She looked up at me. The Shield was cracked, dented, covered in the filth of Isla de la Sangre, but the steel underneath hadn't yielded. She pushed herself up, wincing as her weight shifted onto her bruised hip.

"Dario."

"Stay down."

"No." She grabbed the edge of the radiator and hauled herself to her feet. She swayed, then stabilized. "We fight together. Or we die together. Those are the terms."

I stepped into her space. The air in the cramped supply room smelled of ozone, old grease, and the distinct, copper tang of impending violence. I reached out, my thumb grazing the cut on her cheek. She leaned into the touch, her eyes closing for a fraction of a second.

"You are barely standing," I rasped.

"I don't need to stand to shoot." She opened her eyes. They were dark, dilated, stripping me bare. "How many in the hall?"

"Six. Maybe eight. The heavy hitters."

"Standard formation?"

"They aren't cops, Merritt. They're cleaners. They don't use formations; they use overwhelming force."

I checked the load in my HK45. Three rounds left in the mag. One spare magazine on my belt. A knife in my boot. It wasn't enough. It was never enough.

The door buckled again. The hinges screamed.

Merritt didn't look at the door. She looked at me.

Her gaze dropped to my chest, where the Kevlar vest hung open, the velcro straps torn in the scuffle at the chapel. Underneath, my shirt was soaked through with sweat and blood from the graze on my arm. She stared at the exposed skin, at the corded muscle of my neck, the way my chest heaved with the intake of oxygen.

She reached out, her hand landing flat on my sternum. Her fingers curled, digging into the pectoral muscle, testing the density of it. It wasn't a gentle touch. It was possessive. Hungry.

"You're big," she whispered, her eyes tracking the vein in my bicep as I kept the gun trained on the entry. "I never liked the big ones. Too much ego. Too much space."

"And now?"

She licked her lips. Her pupils blew wide, swallowing the iris. "Now, I look at you and I don't see a man. I see a siege engine. I see walls of muscle built to take punishment so I don't have to."

Her hand slid down my stomach, over the hard ridges of my abs, resting on the heavy buckle of my belt. The heat of her palm seared through the fabric.

"You look like a weapon, Dario," she murmured, a dark appreciation coloring her tone. "Thick. Hard. Capable of absolutely anything. It makes me wet."

The admission hit me harder than a bullet. The lizard brain—the part of me that lived in the gutter and thrived on dominance—roared. Here, at the end of the world, with death hammering at the door, she wanted *me*. Not the intelligence. Not the money. The meat. The violence.

I grabbed her wrist, pressing her hand harder against me.

"I am your weapon," I growled. "Point me."

"The door," she said.

CRASH.

The frame gave way. The door flew inward, kicking up a cloud of plaster dust.

Time slowed. The world narrowed to a tunnel of threat assessment.

Two figures in grey tactical gear surged through the gap. Flashlights blinded us.

I didn't think. I moved.

I took the low line, sliding across the polished concrete. The first mercenary swung his rifle toward me, but he was too slow. I put two rounds into his unarmored pelvis. He folded like a lawn chair.

Merritt fired from behind the radiator. *Crack. Crack.*

Her aim was true. The second man took a round to the throat, just above the ceramic plate of his carrier. He dropped, gurgling.

"Move!" I shouted.

I scrambled up, grabbing the first man's falling rifle—a short-barreled carbine. I didn't check the mag. I turned it on the doorway and held the trigger down.

Suppressing fire. Noise and fury to buy inches of space.

"Go right! The labs!" I roared over the gunfire.

Merritt broke cover. She ran low, a blur of tactical efficiency. I backed her up, walking backward, firing short, controlled bursts into the fatal funnel of the doorway.

Bullets chewed the drywall around my head. Concrete chips stung my face near the eye. I didn't blink.

We hit the corridor.

"Clear left!" Merritt shouted.

"Taking point."

I discarded the empty carbine and switched back to the pistol. We moved down the hall, boots slamming against the linoleum. The facility was waking up. Alarms blared—a rhythmic, deafening klaxon that vibrated in the teeth.

We reached the intersection.

"Contact!"

Three more guards at the far end, near the stairwell. They opened up immediately.

The air snapped. Rounds impacted the wall inches from Merritt's shoulder. She flinched, stumbling.

I grabbed her vest and hauled her around the corner, shielding her body with mine. I felt the dull thud of a round striking my back plate. It knocked the wind out of me, a hammer blow to the kidneys.

"Dario!"

"Armor held," I wheezed. "I'm good."

I wasn't good. My ribs felt like broken glass. But pain was just information, and right now, the information said we were pinned.

We were trapped in a dead-end corridor leading to the chemical processing labs. No exit. Just glass walls and volatile compounds.

"We can't go back," Merritt said, checking her pistol. "Slide lock. I'm dry."

I handed her my spare mag. "Take it."

"What about you?"

"I have the knife."

She hesitated, the metal magazine heavy in her hand. "That leaves you with seven rounds."

"Six," I corrected. "One in the chamber."

She slammed the mag home. "That's suicide math, Ferri."

"It's Italian math. We make it work."

I peaked the corner. Ideally, we would flank. But in a fatal funnel, flanking was a myth. We needed a distraction.

I looked at the fire suppression system running along the ceiling. Heavy pipes. High pressure.

"Can you make that shot?" I pointed to the valve wheel above the guards' heads, fifty yards downrange.

Merritt looked. "Handgun? Fifty yards? Under fire?"

"Yes or no."

She squared her shoulders. The professional mask slid back into place. "Watch me."

She stepped out.

She didn't rush. She adopted a weaver stance, planting her feet, ignoring the rounds snapping past her head. She exhaled.

Bang.

Sparks flew off the pipe. Miss.

"Adjust elevation!" I yelled, firing two rounds to keep their heads down.

Bang.

A jet of white chemical foam exploded from the pipe. It blasted downward with the force of a firehose, engulfing the three guards in a blinding, suffocating cloud.

"Push!" I ordered.

We sprinted.

I hit the foam cloud first. I couldn't see, but I could hear. I heard coughing. The panic of men who couldn't breathe.

I collided with a body. Hard armor.

He swung a fist. I ducked, driving my knife upward into the armpit gap of his vest. He screamed. I ripped the blade free and shoved him away.

A second man stumbled out of the white haze, rubbing his eyes. I pistol-whipped him across the temple. The sound was wet, final. He went down.

The third man was on the floor, retching. Merritt kicked his rifle away and stomped on his wrist.

"Secure," she gasped.

We were through the choke point. But the stairs were blocked by the foam.

"The service hatch," I said, pointing to a heavy steel door marked *BIO-HAZARD*. "It connects to the extraction tunnels."

I tried the handle. Locked. Electronic keypad.

"Damn it." I punched the panel. It chirped a denial.

"Stand back." Merritt raised her gun.

"You can't shoot a mag-lock, Merritt. It's solid steel bolts."

She lowered the weapon. The adrenaline began to fade, replaced by the crushing weight of reality. We were in a hallway. The alarm was still screaming. And we could hear heavy boots on the stairs above us. Reinforcements.

"We're boxed in," she said quietly.

I looked at the door. Then I looked at the vent grate near the floor. Too small for me.

But big enough for her.

The realization sat in my stomach like a stone.

"Merritt." I pointed to the vent.

She looked at it. Then she looked at me. Her face hardened.

"No."

"It leads to the drainage outflow. You can swim to the boat."

"No."

"I can't fit," I said, my voice steady. "But you can."

"I am not leaving you here to die, Dario. We walk out together or we don't walk out."

"Listen to me!" I grabbed her shoulders. I shook her, needing to break through that stubborn, federal pride. "This isn't a negotiation.

The mission is the children. If you don't pilot that boat, they don't leave Mexican waters. They die. Is that what you want?"

"The pilot—"

"Is a coward. He'll run at the first sign of a cutter. You have the badge. You have the authority. You have to get them home."

Tears welled in her eyes. Hot, angry tears. "And what do you have?"

"I have a knife," I said, thumbing the blade. "And a very bad temper."

The boots were louder now. Just around the landing.

"Dario..." Her voice cracked.

I pulled her in. I kissed her. It wasn't soft. I tasted blood and salt and desperation. I kissed her like I wanted to imprint my soul onto her mouth, so that wherever she went, she would taste me.

I broke the kiss, resting my forehead against hers.

"Go," I whispered. "Be the Shield."

She stared at me for one agonizing heartbeat. Then she nodded. A jerk of the chin. Acceptance.

She dropped to her knees and kicked the grate in. She shimmied into the dark, narrow space.

She looked back once. Her face was framed by the galvanized steel, a portrait of heartbreak.

"If you die," she hissed, "I will never forgive you."

"Go!"

She disappeared into the dark.

I stood up. I adjusted my vest. I wiped the blood from my eyes.

I turned to face the corridor. The foam was settling. Through the haze, I saw shadows moving. Five. Ten.

I checked my pistol. Four rounds.

Perfect.

I stepped out into the center of the hall. I wasn't hiding anymore. I wasn't running.

I was the wall.

"Come and get it," I whispered.

I raised the gun.

And for the first time in my life, standing alone in the dark, I wasn't afraid.

Because she was safe. And they had to go through hell to get to her.

I was Hell.

CHAPTER SIXTEEN

A LIE COMPOSED OF TRUTHS

The diesel fumes taste like him.

Salt spray and heavy, unrefined fuel. It coats my throat, a phantom gag reflex that has nothing to do with the chop of the waves and everything to do with the emptiness beside me.

The throttle vibrates under my palm. My hand is numb, the knuckles skinned raw and packed with grime from the island, but I don't let go. If I let go, the boat stops. If the boat stops, the silence catches up.

Behind me, in the cabin, the children are quiet. Too quiet. They are small, huddled shapes wrapped in thermal blankets, staring at nothing. They don't cry. They don't ask for their mothers. El Santo burned the questions out of them, leaving only a hollow obedience.

I check the compass. North-Northwest.

I don't look back.

Looking back means acknowledging the pillar of black smoke smearing the horizon. Looking back means admitting that the man who branded his soul onto mine in a storm-battered bunker is standing alone in a room full of fire and bullets.

Go, he said. *Be the Shield.*

My chest aches. A physical, crushing pressure behind the sternum. It isn't the bruised ribs from the fight. It's the severance. It's the terrifying realization that for the last seventy-two hours, I haven't been an Agent. I haven't been a Shield. I was a woman untethered, and he was the gravity holding me to the earth.

Now gravity is gone. And I am drifting.

The phantom weight of his hand on the back of my neck lingers—heat, calluses, the absolute possession of his grip. My body remembers the violence of his mouth, the worship in his touch, the way he stripped me down to the marrow and found something worth saving.

Dario.

The name is a jagged stone in my throat.

Lights appear on the horizon. San Diego. The Coronado Bridge creates a sparkling arc against the dawn sky. It looks clean. Orderly.

Civilization.

I hate it.

I throttle down. The engine pitch drops from a roar to a growl. We drift toward the marina, the hull slapping against the wake.

Blue lights flash on the pier. Not the erratic strobe of a crime scene, but the synchronized, rhythmic pulse of a containment zone. Black SUVs. Men in suits standing in rigid lines.

No ambulances. No trauma teams for the children.

Just the clean-up crew.

I dock the boat. My legs threaten to buckle as I step onto the wood, the land rolling beneath me like a liquid.

"Federal Agent!" I croak. My voice is wrecked, shredded by smoke. "I have eleven minors. Victims of trafficking. They need medical—"

Two men in dark suits intercept me. They don't offer hands to help. They flank me. Hard stops.

"Agent Gage," the one on the left says. He wears an earpiece and a tie that costs more than my car. "Director Halloway is waiting."

"The kids," I snap, trying to push past him. "Get the medics."

"The children are being processed. Secure transport is arranged."

"Processed? They need a hospital!"

"They need to be debriefed. This is a matter of national security."

He grabs my arm.

The touch is wrong. It's bureaucratic. Sterile. It breaks the skin-memory of Dario's rough, desperate hold on me.

I jerk away. "Don't touch me."

"The car, Agent Gage."

I look at the SUVs. The windows are tinted black, reflecting my own face back at me—a stranger with hollow cheeks, blood in her hair, and eyes that have seen the end of the world.

I look back at the boat. The kids are being herded into a van. Efficient. Silent. Like product moving from one warehouse to another.

The System isn't here to help. It's here to reset.

I get in the car.

*

The interrogation room is white.

No windows. No clock. Just the hum of the HVAC system pumping recycled air into a box designed to strip away time. The table is bolted to the floor. The chair is cold metal.

I sit. My hands rest on the table. They are shaking. Not a tremble, but a high-frequency vibration I can't stop. I clasp them together, white-knuckling my own fingers to hide the weakness.

The door opens.

Director Halloway walks in. He looks exactly as he did the day he recruited me ten years ago—grey suit, silver hair, the face of a grandfather who signs death warrants with a fountain pen.

He carries a file. He sits opposite me. He doesn't offer water.

"Merritt," he says. His voice is soft, paternal. "You look like hell."

"I found it," I say. The words tumble out, hard and fast. "The island. The testing ground. They were conditioning children, Halloway. Turning them into sleepers. I have the location. I have the survivors."

Halloway opens the file. He stares at the papers, not at me.

"We have the children, yes. Poor things. Found drifting in Mexican waters."

"I brought them in. I raided the facility."

"The report says you suffered a mental break after the death of Agent Reynolds." Halloway turns a page. "That you went AWOL. That you hijacked a civilian vessel and disappeared into cartel territory."

The air leaves the room.

"I went rogue because you wouldn't sign the warrant," I say, my voice dropping to a dangerous register. "I found Jack's killers. I found the pipeline."

"You found a gang hideout," Halloway corrects. "A tragic squalor. Drugs. Local violence."

"It wasn't drugs! It was mind control. It was industrial-scale trafficking. Dario Ferri—"

"Dario Ferri is a known organized crime figure," Halloway cuts in. "A murderer. A predator. And you were seen conspiring with him."

"He helped me. He saved those kids."

"Did he?" Halloway looks up. His eyes are flat, grey coins. "Or did he manipulate a grieving, unstable federal agent into eliminating his competition?"

The gaslight flares. It burns hot and bright.

"I know what I saw," I whisper. "I saw the cages. I saw the logs."

"Logs?" Halloway pauses.

"The shipping manifests. The orders."

A muscle feathers in Halloway's jaw. A microscopic tell.

"And where are these logs, Merritt?"

"Ferri has them."

"Ah." Halloway leans back. A small, pitying smile touches his lips. "So the mobster has the evidence. Convenient."

"He stayed behind to destroy the facility. To buy us time."

"To destroy the evidence, you mean."

My blood turns cold. It's a slow, creeping frost that starts in my toes and works its way up to my heart.

"You're burying it," I realize. "Why?"

Halloway sighs. He closes the file.

"The geopolitical situation is delicate, Merritt. We are negotiating new trade agreements. Border security funding is on the ballot. We cannot have a scandal involving... exotic theories about conditioning camps."

"Exotic theories? I brought you the victims!"

"The victims are confused. Trauma messes with memory. They'll be treated. Silent professionals will help them forget."

"Like you helped me forget Jack?"

Halloway stands up. He walks to the mirror. He adjusts his tie.

"Jack Reynolds was a good man. But he asked too many questions about things above his pay grade. Just like you."

"Who?" I demand. "Who are you protecting?"

Halloway turns. "We protect the institution, Merritt. Stability."

"It's Julian, isn't it?"

The name hangs in the air between us. A grenade with the pin pulled.

Halloway doesn't flinch. He doesn't blink. But the temperature in the room drops ten degrees.

"Councilman Vance is a pillar of this community," Halloway says softly. "He is grieving the loss of his brother-in-law. He has been very concerned about your... stability. He pulled a lot of strings to keep you out of federal prison today."

The puzzle pieces slam together. The sound is deafening inside my skull.

Jack finding the discrepancies. Jack trying to talk to Julian. Julian, the grieving politician, holding my hand at the funeral, feeding me lies about gang violence while he signed the manifests that shipped children into hell.

He used me. He used my grief as a blindfold.

And Halloway is the janitor.

A dark, cold clarity washes over me. The shaking in my hands stops.

They think I am broken. They think I am a hysterical woman who fell for a mobster and lost her mind in the jungle.

They are wrong.

I am not the Shield anymore. The Shield protects. The Shield deflects.

I don't want to deflect. I want to shatter.

"Where is he?" I ask. My voice is steady. Flat.

Halloway looks confused. "Who?"

"Ferri. Is he in custody?"

Halloway's expression shifts. The pity returns, but this time, it's mixed with a cruel finality.

"Merritt," he says. "The facility exploded. The Mexican Marines swept the site an hour ago."

"He's alive," I say. "He's too mean to die."

"There was a firefight. The cartel reinforcements... they didn't take prisoners."

"Show me."

Halloway hesitates. Then he reaches into his breast pocket. He pulls out a single, glossy photograph. He slides it across the metal table.

It skids to a stop in front of me.

I look down.

The world tilts on its axis.

It's an arm. A muscular, scarred forearm protruding from a pile of rubble and rebar. The skin is grey, coated in dust.

But the tattoo is clear. The intricate, black ink of the double-headed eagle, the Ferri family crest.

And on the wrist, a watch. The Breitling emergency beacon. The crystal is shattered. The hands are frozen.

But it isn't the watch that rips the scream from my throat.

It's the hand itself.

The fingers are curled tight, locked in a rigor of final defiance. And clutched in the fist, glinting in the harsh flash of the forensic camera, is a silver chain.

My St. Christopher medal.

I gave it to him in the bunker. *To guide you back,* I had whispered against his skin.

He held onto it. He held onto it while the roof came down. He held onto it instead of a weapon.

My lungs turn to stone. The room shrinks to the size of a coffin.

"The blast collapsed the catacombs," Halloway says, his voice coming from a thousand miles away. "There were no survivors in the lower levels. I'm sorry, Merritt."

He's gone.

The Sword is broken.

The only man who ever saw me—who saw the monster beneath the badge and loved it—is buried under a mountain of concrete and lies.

I stare at the photo. I stare until the image burns into my retinas.

Halloway puts a hand on my shoulder.

"Go home, Merritt. Take some leave. Let Julian take care of you. He wants to help you heal."

Let the murderer take care of the widow.

I stand up. My chair scrapes loudly against the floor.

I don't look at Halloway. I pick up the photo. I fold it carefully and place it in my pocket, right against my heart, where the heat of Dario's hand used to be.

"I'm resigning," I say.

"That's for the best," Halloway nods. "Clean break."

I walk to the door. I pause, my hand on the knob.

"You're right, Director," I say. I turn to look at him. My eyes are dry. My soul is a smoking crater. "Trauma changes people."

"It does."

"It clears the vision."

I open the door and walk out into the sterile, fluorescent hallway. I don't run. I don't cry.

I walk with the rhythm of a woman who has nothing left to lose, and a war to start.

Julian Vance killed my husband. He sold children. And he buried the only man who could have stopped him.

He thinks the story is over. He thinks the Shield is broken.

He forgot that when a shield breaks, it leaves jagged edges. I am going to sharpen them. And then I am going to cut his throat.

CHAPTER SEVENTEEN

WHITE WALLS, WET CEMENT

The water in the basin was cold. I splashed it over my face, but it didn't wash away the grime of the last forty-eight hours. It didn't wash away the lie Halloway had planted in my chest like a tumor.

He's gone.

I gripped the porcelain edges of the sink until the ceramic groaned under the pressure. The face in the mirror wasn't mine. It belonged to a ghost. Hollow cheeks, eyes rimmed in red, lips cracked from dehydration. I was a shell, emptied out and left to rot in a government-subsidized apartment while the men who built the slaughterhouse drank scotch in climate-controlled offices.

The photograph sat on the edge of the vanity.

I hated it. I needed it.

It was the only piece of him left. A glossy, high-resolution image of an arm protruding from a pile of rebar and concrete. Grey dust coated the skin. Red blood pooled in the shadows. The Ferri crest—the double-headed eagle—was visible through the debris.

And the hand. The fist clenched in rigor mortis, holding the silver St. Christopher medal.

I picked it up. My fingers trembled.

I had memorized the image in the interrogation room, but here, in the silence of my bathroom, under the harsh glare of the vanity bulbs, it looked different.

I traced the line of the wrist. The watch. Broken. Stopped at 4:12 AM. The time of the blast.

Perfect. Too perfect.

I leaned in closer. My breath fogged the mirror, but I didn't wipe it away. I focused on the thumb.

The memory hit me with the force of a physical blow.

The bunker. The smell of ozone and sweat. Dario's hand on my throat, grounding me while the world burned outside. My tongue tracing the ridge of scar tissue on his right thumb—a jagged, white line from a knife fight in Naples he'd told me about in a whisper. Use your teeth, he'd said. Make it real.

I remembered the texture of that scar. Hard. Raised. A flaw in the marble.

I looked at the photo.

The thumb clutching the medal was dirty. It was bloody.

But the skin was smooth.

There was no scar. No ridge. No history.

My heart stopped. For a full second, the blood ceased to move in my veins. Then it slammed back into motion, hot and violent.

This wasn't Dario's hand.

It was a prop. A dead sicario pulled from the pile, dressed in a watch, painted with a tattoo, and posed with a medal they must have taken from him before the collapse.

They staged it.

Halloway didn't just bury the truth; he manufactured a corpse to keep me quiet. He needed me broken. He needed me grieving. Because a grieving woman hides in her room, but an angry woman burns cities.

I dropped the photo. It fluttered into the wet sink. The water began to warp the paper, dissolving the lie.

"You stupid son of a bitch," I whispered.

The despair evaporated. The cold, heavy stone in my chest cracked open, and something molten poured out.

He was alive.

If they went to this much trouble to fake his death, he wasn't just a loose end. He was leverage. They were holding him. They were squeezing him for the ledger, for the codes, for the locations I hadn't given them.

I checked my watch. Six hours since the "extraction."

If he was alive, he was suffering. Dario wouldn't talk. He would let them peel the skin from his bones before he gave them the satisfaction of a scream.

I wasn't an ICE Agent anymore. I wasn't a Shield.

I walked out of the bathroom. I didn't pack clothes. I didn't pack food.

I went to the vent in the floor of my closet. I pried it open.

Inside lay the "incidental" kit I had kept hidden from Jack, from Halloway, from everyone. A Glock 19 with the serial numbers filed off. Three magazines of hollow points. A ceramic knife. A burner phone.

I racked the slide. The sound was a promise.

Julian Vance had a logistics hub near the port. A "secure" warehouse for his import/export business. The same business that moved children like cargo. If they were holding a high-value target like Dario, they wouldn't take him to a federal prison. They would take him to the pipeline.

I shoved the gun into my waistband.

I walked to the door. I caught my reflection in the hallway mirror one last time.

The ghost was gone. The monster was back.

The warehouse sat on the edge of the bleak industrial sprawl of the Port of San Diego. It was a monolith of corrugated steel and shadow, surrounded by a chain-link fence topped with razor wire that gleamed under the floodlights.

"Vance Logistics."

The name was painted in blue, cheerful letters on the side of the building.

I killed the headlights of the stolen sedan a block away. I approached on foot, moving through the dead space of the shipping container stacks. The air smelled of diesel and brine.

Two guards at the gate. Private military. Paladin Global. They wore grey fatigues and carried carbines, standing with the bored arrogance of men who knew the local cops were on the payroll.

I didn't have time for stealth. I had rage.

I moved to the blind spot of the camera tower. I picked up a rock and tossed it against the metal siding of a dumpster. *Clang.*

The guard on the left turned. "Check it."

He walked into the shadows.

I stepped out behind him. I didn't use the gun. I used the knife.

I drove the ceramic blade into the soft spot between his helmet and his vest. He dropped without a sound, his nervous system severed. I dragged him into the dark.

The second guard was checking his phone. He looked up when I stepped into the light.

He saw a woman in jeans and a black hoodie. He hesitated.

"Hey, you can't be—"

I put a bullet in his knee.

He screamed, dropping his rifle. As he fell, I stepped in and kicked him in the chest, knocking the wind out of him. I knelt, pressing the hot muzzle of the Glock against his tear duct.

"Where is he?"

"Who?" he wheezed.

"The prisoner. The Italian."

"I don't know what—"

I shifted the aim to his other knee.

"Basement!" he shrieked. "The heat exchanger room! Level B-2!"

"Keycard."

He fumbled for the lanyard at his belt. I ripped it off his neck.

"Sleep," I said.

I pistol-whipped him. He went limp.

I strode toward the main doors. The gunshot would have alerted the interior. Good. I wanted them to know I was coming. I wanted them to be afraid.

I swiped the card. The heavy steel door hissed open.

Alarm klaxons began to wail.

I entered the facility.

It was a maze of conveyor belts and crates. High above, catwalks crisscrossed the ceiling. Shadows moved.

"Contact front!" a voice yelled from the gantry.

Bullets sparked off the concrete floor near my feet.

I didn't take cover. I moved forward, firing. I was a machine of efficient violence. I tracked the muzzle flashes. *Bang. Bang.*

A body fell from the catwalk, landing with a wet thud on a pallet of crates.

I pushed deeper. I found the freight elevator. I hit the button for B-2.

The doors opened.

Three men in lab coats and tactical vests waited in the corridor. They raised their weapons.

I dropped to a knee, making myself a small target. I fired a controlled pair into the center mass of the first man, then snapped the aim to the head of the second. The third man turned to run. I shot him in the spine.

I stepped over them. The air grew hotter as I descended the corridor. The hum of industrial machinery vibrated in my teeth.

Heat exchanger room.

The door was reinforced steel. No window.

I swiped the card. Access denied.

"Open it," I commanded the lock.

It beeped red.

I stepped back. I aimed at the hinges. It wouldn't open it, but it would weaken the integrity. I fired three rounds into the top hinge, three into the bottom.

Then I ran at the door and kicked it with everything I had.

The metal groaned and buckled inward.

I squeezed through the gap.

The room was a sauna. Steam hissed from overhead pipes. In the center of the room, bolted to a chair that looked like it belonged in an inquisition, was a man.

Dario.

He was stripped to the waist. His body was a map of fresh violence—bruises blooming purple and black against the olive skin, cuts weeping blood. His head hung low, chin resting on his chest.

A man in a plastic apron stood over him, holding a pair of heavy pliers.

The torturer turned, surprised by the intrusion. He raised the tool like a weapon.

I didn't hesitate. I put a bullet through his eye.

He dropped.

The room went silent, save for the hiss of steam and the ragged sound of breathing.

"Dario."

My voice cracked. It was the first time I had spoken his name aloud since the island.

The figure in the chair stirred. He lifted his head slowly, fighting the gravity of pain. One eye was swollen shut. The other was bloodshot, wild, animalistic.

He focused on me.

For a second, he didn't recognize me. He expected another demon. Then, the recognition hit. The tension left his shoulders, replaced by a shock so profound it looked like agony.

"Merritt?"

His voice was a ruin. Gravel and glass.

I holstered the gun. I ran to him. I fell to my knees between his spread legs, my hands hovering over his battered chest, afraid to touch him, afraid I would break him.

"I'm here," I choked out. "I'm here."

"You... left," he rasped. A ghost of a smile touched his split lip. "You followed orders."

"I followed a lie."

I reached for the restraints. heavy plastic zip-ties bit into his wrists, cutting off circulation. His hands were dark, swollen.

"Hold still."

I pulled the ceramic knife from my boot. I slid the blade between the plastic and his skin. I saw the damage then—the raw, flayed skin where he had fought the bindings. The broken fingers.

I cut the ties. One. Two.

His arms fell to his sides. He didn't have the strength to lift them.

"Can you walk?" I asked, grabbing his face gently to look into his eye.

"For you?" He coughed, spitting blood onto the concrete. "I can run."

He leaned forward, resting his forehead against mine. He was burning up. His skin radiated a fever heat that seared me.

"I thought you were dead," I whispered. "They showed me... a photo."

"They tried," he muttered against my skin. "They wanted the ledger codes. They wanted to know where you went."

"What did you tell them?"

The corner of his mouth twitched. The old arrogance flared behind the pain. "I told them to go to hell. And that my wife would send them there shortly."

The word hit me. *Wife.* A claim. A title. Not legal, but binding in blood.

I pulled back. I looked at his hands.

And there it was. On his right thumb. The jagged white scar. The flaw I had looked for in the mirror.

I brought his hand to my mouth. I kissed the scar. I tasted the blood and the sweat and the iron of him.

"Let's go home, Dario."

He gripped my shoulder. His strength was returning, fed by the proximity of the Shield.

"Not home," he growled. He used my body as a crutch to haul himself upright. He swayed, then locked his knees. He looked down at the dead torturer, then at the door where the sirens were getting louder.

"We have work to do."

I slipped my arm around his waist, taking his weight. He was heavy, solid, real.

"Julian," I said.

"Julian," he agreed.

He reached down and took the pistol from my waistband. He checked the chamber with a practiced, lethal motion, despite his broken fingers.

He looked at me. The predator was back.

"Lead the way, Agent Gage."

I turned toward the door. The world outside wanted to bury us. It wanted to edit us out of the story.

Let them try.

We walked out of the steam and into the fire, together.

"Clear left," I said.

"Clear right," he answered.

We moved as one organism. The Sword and the Shield.

And we were just getting started.

CHAPTER EIGHTEEN

KINETIC THERAPY

The heavy steel door slammed shut, severing the sight line to the hallway and the three bodies we left cooling on the linoleum. I dropped the locking bar into place. The metal clanged—a sound of finality that echoed in the cramped space.

"Clear," I rasped. My throat felt like I'd swallowed a handful of glass.

Dario didn't answer immediately. He leaned against a rack of industrial shelving, his chest heaving. The air in the supply bunker smelled of ozone, gun oil, and the copper tang of his blood. Outside, the alarm klaxons continued their rhythmic, deafening scream, but in here, the noise was muffled, distant.

We were trapped. The warehouse was swarming with Paladin mercenaries. Julian's private army.

I turned to face him.

The emergency lighting painted the room in sickly yellow hues, but even in the bad light, Dario Ferri was a masterpiece of wreckage. He had stripped to the waist during the torture session, and now, standing amidst the crates of illicit cargo, he looked less like a man and more like a weapon that had been fired until the barrel glowed white-hot.

I stepped closer. My hands, still shaking from the adrenaline dump of the rescue, reached out to hover over his ribs.

"Sit down," I ordered. "I need to check the damage."

"I'm fine," he grunted. He tried to straighten, but a grimace twisted his mouth. He slid down the shelving unit until he hit the concrete floor, his legs sprawling out.

I dropped to my knees between his thighs. The intimacy of the position didn't register as sexual, not yet. It was tactical. I needed access to the wounds.

"They worked you over," I said quietly. My fingers traced the fresh, purple bruising blooming across his oblique muscles. "Pliers?"

"And a cattle prod," he said. His voice was rough, a low rumble that vibrated through the floorplate and into my knees. "They wanted the encryption keys for the ledger."

"Did you give them anything?"

He looked at me then. His left eye was swollen shut, a grotesque shade of plum, but the right eye was clear. It burned with a cold, terrifying intelligence.

"I gave them a promise," he said. "That you were coming."

The confession hit me harder than a physical blow. He had waited in the dark, enduring agony, banking on the absolute certainty that I would burn the city down to find him.

"I almost didn't," I whispered. I unclipped the med-kit from my belt. "Halloway... he showed me a photo. A dead body with your tattoo."

"Halloway is a clerk. Clerks think paperwork defines reality." Dario flinched as I pressed an antiseptic wipe against a deep gash on his shoulder. "You and I... we write in blood."

I cleaned the wound. The silence stretched between us, heavy and charged. The danger outside was a physical weight pressing against the door, but the danger inside was sharper. It was the proximity. It was the heat radiating off his skin.

I finished bandaging the shoulder. I sat back on my heels, wiping my hands on my jeans.

I looked at him. Really looked at him.

God, he was beautiful. Not in the way a model is beautiful, all symmetry and softness. He was beautiful like a cliff face battered by the ocean. His torso was a map of survival. Ropes of muscle coiled under his olive skin, hard and defined, twitching with the aftershocks of pain. A vein pulsed in his neck, thick and steady. The dark hair on his chest was matted with sweat and dried blood, leading down to the V-taper of his hips where his tactical pants hung low, held up by a heavy leather belt.

He was massive. He took up all the air in the room. Even broken, sitting on the floor of a bunker, he projected a lethality that made my mouth water. He was kinetic energy trapped in skin.

My gaze dropped to his hands—large, scarred, brutal hands that had snapped necks and signed death warrants. And yet, those same hands had held me while I fell apart in a safehouse. They had worshipped me.

The hunger hit me then. Sudden. Violent.

It wasn't a desire for comfort. It was a need to consume.

I wanted to lick the blood off his skin. I wanted to feel the weight of him crushing the air out of my lungs, proving that we were still here, still solid.

Dario watched me watching him. A corner of his mouth lifted—not a smile, but a predator's acknowledgment of prey entering the clearing.

"See something you like, Agent Gage?"

"I see a mess," I lied. My voice dropped an octave. "I see a liability."

"Liar."

He reached out. His hand, the one with the broken fingers splinted with tape, wrapped around the back of my neck. He didn't pull. He just held me there, his thumb stroking the sensitive skin behind my ear. The callus against my skin sent a jolt of electricity straight to my groin.

"You're looking at me like you want to finish what they started," he murmured.

"Maybe I do."

I leaned in. The space between us evaporated. I could smell him—musk, iron, the sharp tang of antiseptic. It was the most intoxicating thing I had ever smelled.

"We have maybe ten minutes before they blow that door," I said.

"Plenty of time," he rasped.

He pulled.

I went willingly. I crashed into him, my mouth finding his.

The kiss wasn't gentle. It was a collision of teeth and desperation. He tasted of blood and mint and fury. I groaned, the sound torn from my throat, and straddled his lap properly, grinding my hips down against the hard ridge of his erection.

He hissed—pain mixed with pleasure—but his grip on my neck tightened.

"Careful," he growled against my lips. "Ribs."

"I don't care about your ribs," I muttered, biting his lower lip hard enough to draw fresh blood. "I care about this. Being alive."

I pulled back just enough to look at him. His good eye was blown wide, the pupil swallowing the iris. The mask of the stoic Don was gone. This was just the man. The animal.

"Take it off," he ordered.

I stood up. I didn't fumble. I stripped off the hoodie, then the tank top. My bra followed. I stood before him in the yellow light, bare from the waist up, my skin flushed, my nipples hard points of sensation in the cool air.

He didn't touch me. He just looked. His gaze felt like a physical caress, heavy and possessive, tracing the curve of my breasts, the scars on my stomach, the gun tucked into my waistband.

"Perfect," he whispered. A reverence reserved for holy relics and loaded weapons.

I shucked my jeans. I kicked them aside.

I stood in my panties, weaponless, shieldless.

"You're mine," he said. It wasn't a question. It was a statement of fact, etched into the stone of the earth.

"Prove it."

I dropped to my knees again. I went for his belt. The buckle was heavy, cold metal. My fingers worked quickly, desperate, clumsy with lust. I freed him.

He sprang free, thick and heavy, twitching against his stomach.

I didn't wait. I didn't tease. We didn't have time for foreplay. The Reaper was knocking at the door, and I intended to scream in his face.

I climbed onto him. I positioned myself.

He grabbed my hips. His fingers dug into my flesh, bruising, grounding.

"Look at me," he commanded.

I looked.

"Merritt."

He thrust up.

I gasped, throwing my head back as he filled me. It was a shock to the system—a blunt, invading force that stretched me, filled me, claimed me. He was huge, unyielding, and absolutely magnificent.

I sank down until I was flush against him. We fit together like two pieces of a broken world snapping back into place.

For a second, we didn't move. We just breathed, syncing our lungs, syncing our hearts. The vibration of the alarms outside faded into white noise.

Then he moved.

He snapped his hips upward, driving deep, hitting a spot that made my vision blur.

"Dario," I choked out.

"I'm here," he grunted, matching my rhythm. "Right here."

It wasn't making love. It was kinetic therapy. It was two survivors trying to merge their cells so they couldn't be torn apart again. I rode him with a frantic energy, my hands braced on his broad, sweat-slicked shoulders, my nails digging into his skin.

He met every thrust with a growl, his hand sliding up to cup my breast, his thumb flicking over the nipple, sending spikes of pleasure radiating through my chest.

"You saved me," he rasped, his voice wrecked. "You came back."

"I'll always come back," I panted. "You're my partner."

"More," he corrected. He grabbed my hair, pulling my head back, exposing my throat. He buried his face in the crook of my neck, biting down on the pulse point. "More."

"Yes."

The friction built. It was a fire in my belly, a tightening coil that wound tighter and tighter with every slap of skin against skin, every ragged breath. I needed the release. I needed the oblivion.

He sensed it. He knew my body better than I did. He switched his grip to my waist, locking me down, dictating the pace. Hard. Fast. Brutal.

"Let go," he ordered.

I shattered.

The climax hit me like a train wreck. My body seized, pleasure arcing through my nerves, blinding and white-hot. I cried out, a raw, animal sound that I didn't try to stifle. I clamped down on him, milking him, shaking apart in his arms.

He followed me seconds later. He groaned, a deep, guttural roar of release, his body bowing off the floor as he poured himself into me.

We stayed like that for a long time. Collapsed against each other. Sweating. Panting. My heart hammered against his chest, a frantic drumbeat slowing to a steady rhythm.

The room was quiet again, save for the distant wail of the sirens.

Slowly, reality began to bleed back in.

Dario shifted. He kissed my shoulder. A soft, lingering touch that contrasted sharply with the violence of the last few minutes.

"You okay?" he asked.

I rested my forehead against his. "I'm alive."

"Good."

He helped me up. He didn't look away as I dressed. He watched me pull the armor of my clothes back on, his expression unreadable but intense.

I tossed him his shirt. He winced as he pulled it on, hiding the map of bruises, but the movement was fluid. Efficient.

He stood up. He checked the magazine of the pistol I had given him. He racked the slide.

The lover was gone. The Capo was back.

"Julian," he said. The name was a curse.

"He's in the penthouse office," I said, checking my own weapon. "Top floor. Logistics oversight."

Dario walked to the door. He placed his hand on the locking bar. He looked back at me.

"Ready to burn it down?"

I looked at the man who had just claimed my soul in a supply closet. I looked at the gun in my hand. I thought about the children on the boat. I thought about Jack.

I felt cold. Hard. Diamond-sharp.

"Open it," I said.

Dario lifted the bar.

He kicked the door open.

We stepped out into the hallway, weapons raised, leaving the sanctuary behind.

The world wanted a war. We were about to give it one.

CHAPTER NINETEEN

THE NEW GEOMETRY

The door swung open, and the world dissolved into noise.

The warehouse floor was a twisted grid of shipping containers and shadows, a chaotic geometry designed to hide illicit cargo. Now, it was a kill box. The klaxons were deafening, a rhythmic scream that vibrated in the fillings of my teeth, but beneath that mechanical wail, I tracked the heavier thud of boots on concrete.

"Move," Dario growled.

He didn't wait for me. He surged past, moving with a predator's grace despite the bruised ribs and the tape binding his broken fingers. He raised the pistol I'd given him, cleared the corner of a crate, and fired. Two shots. Controlled. Efficient.

A guard dropped from the catwalk above, his rifle clattering against the metal railing before he hit the ground with a wet crunch.

My heart didn't hammer; it seized, holding a steady, painful rhythm against my sternum. Fear was a luxury I couldn't afford. Fear belonged to the woman who used to wear a badge and wait for backup. That woman died on the island.

We moved into the open lane.

"Contact!" a voice shouted from the gantry.

Bullets chewed up the concrete inches from my boot. Concrete dust sprayed my shins.

I didn't flinch. I raised the Glock. I didn't see a man; I saw a target acquisition profile. Center mass. The recoil jarred my wrist, a familiar, grounding shock. I hammered a volley at the suppression team on the upper rail. One man folded over the guardrail. The others ducked.

"Right flank," I shouted, my voice raw.

Dario was already there. He used a forklift as cover, firing through the gap in the protective cage. He was a creature of kinetic violence, his movements sharp and economical. Every bullet he spent purchased us another second of life.

We advanced. We weren't hiding anymore. We were cutting a path.

The air grew thick with smoke and the acrid stench of cordite. It burned my eyes, but I didn't blink. I kept my focus on the freight elevator at the far end of the facility. The only way up. The only way to Julian.

A Paladin mercenary stepped out from behind a stack of crates, leveling a submachine gun. He was ten feet away. Too close.

The barrel swung toward Dario.

"No," I hissed.

I didn't shoot. I slammed my shoulder into Dario, knocking him off balance and into the cover of a steel pillar. I took the space he had occupied. The mercenary fired.

The air snapped past my ear. Heat scorched my cheek.

I drove forward, closing the distance before he could adjust his aim. I grabbed the barrel of his weapon with my off-hand, ignoring the searing heat of the metal, and drove the ceramic knife into his throat.

He gurgled. His eyes went wide, the pupils blowing out in shock.

I ripped the blade free. He crumpled.

Dario was at my side instantly. He grabbed my arm, his grip bruising. He checked me for holes. His eyes were wild, the iris almost swallowed by the black of his pupils.

"Don't you ever," he snarled, winded and furious, "put yourself in front of a bullet for me."

"I'm the Shield," I panted, wiping blood splatter from my jaw. "Do your job. Be the Sword."

He looked at me. For a split second, the violence around us suspended. He didn't see an agent. He saw the monster he had helped create. A dark approval twisted his mouth.

"Then shield me," he said.

We moved again.

The resistance thickened near the elevator. They knew where we were going. Julian was up there, likely watching on the monitors, sipping scotch while he waited for his paid killers to wipe us off the ledger.

We took cover behind a generator. Bullets sparked off the casing.

"Cover me," Dario ordered.

He broke cover. He didn't run away from the fire; he ran perpendicular to it, drawing their eyes, drawing their aim. It was suicide. It was magnificent.

I popped up. Three guards were tracking him. Their backs were to me.

I took the shots. One. Two. Three.

Dario reached the elevator control panel. He smashed the call button with the butt of his pistol, then turned and fired blindly into the shadows to keep head down.

The heavy steel doors groaned open.

"Clear!" he shouted.

We scrambled inside. I hit the button for the Penthouse. The doors hissed shut, cutting off the deafening roar of the gunfight, sealing us in a sudden, ringing silence.

The elevator began to rise.

The box was small. Mirrors lined the walls, reflecting us back at ourselves—two blood-soaked ghosts breathing hard, smelling of sweat and murder.

I looked at him. His chest heaved. Fresh blood seeped through his shirt where the stitches on his shoulder had torn. He was barely standing, running on pure, uncut hate.

Adrenaline crashed into my system. It wasn't the flight response. It was the other thing. The life drive. The desperate need to affirm existence in the face of inevitable death.

My gaze snapped to his hands. Blood crusted the knuckles. Hands that killed. Hands that destroyed.

I needed them on me.

I slammed him against the mirrored wall. The glass groaned under the impact.

"Merritt," he growled, a warning that sounded like a plea.

I silenced him with teeth. I crushed my mouth to his, biting his lower lip until fresh blood bloomed. Iron and salt hit my tongue. Primal. There was no romance here, just the desperate hunger of two animals still breathing.

He dropped his gun. The heavy thud echoed like a gavel.

His grip bruised my hips as he hauled me up. I wrapped my legs around his waist, my thighs clamping down hard, muscles coiling tight.

"You're fucking insane," he rasped, his hand tearing at the waistband of my tactical pants.

"Fuck me," I hissed. "Right now."

He didn't hesitate. He freed himself, thick and furious. He shoved aside the fabric of my panties, his fingers grazing my clit, finding me already soaked. My body had betrayed me, slick with anticipation despite the slaughter below.

He lined up and drove home.

One thrust. He buried his cock deep inside my pussy, stretching me, filling me completely.

My head cracked back against the mirror. A gasp tore from my throat, raw and needy.

He grabbed my hair, pulling my neck back to expose the throat. "Take it," he snarled.

He pounded into me. Rough. Merciless. The friction was electric, a fire lighting up my nerve endings. He hit my cervix, that deep, aching spot that made my toes curl and my vision blur. We were ascending in a metal coffin, but I felt alive. Indestructible.

"Mine," he roared, driving harder. "You submit to this. Only this."

"Yes," I choked out. "Harder."

My pussy clamped around him, milking him, begging for his seed. I needed to feel him ruin me. The pleasure spiked, blinding and white-hot. I shrieked as I came, my body convulsing, locking him in.

He stiffened, veins bulging in his neck. He bottomed out, grinding his hips against mine.

He erupted.

Hot, thick ropes of cum shot deep inside me. He pumped into my womb, flooding me, claiming me from the inside out. He didn't pull back; he held me there, filling me until I was overflowing.

We hung there for a heartbeat, ragged and ruined, twitching in the afterglow of violence.

Then, the bell dinged.

Level P. Penthouse.

Reality slammed back into place.

Dario dropped me to my feet. He didn't say a word. He bent down, retrieved his weapon, and racked the slide. He wiped the blood from his mouth with the back of his hand.

I adjusted my clothes. I pulled the Glock from my waistband.

I looked at the reflection in the mirror one last time. My lips were swollen. My eyes were wild.

I locked the pleasure away in a steel box in the back of my mind. I would examine it later, if we survived. Right now, I needed to be sharp.

The doors opened.

The penthouse lobby was a violent contrast to the slaughter below. White marble floors. Modern art. Quiet efficiency.

Two men in suits stood by the reception desk. Paladin elite detail.

They reached for their weapons inside their jackets. Slow. So slow.

Dario took the one on the left. I took the one on the right.

Bang. Bang.

They dropped before they cleared leather.

We stepped over the bodies. The double doors to Julian's office loomed ahead. Mahogany. Heavy. Expensive.

Dario looked at me. He nodded at the door.

"Together," he said.

"Together," I answered.

He kicked the door. It flew open, slamming against the interior wall.

We walked in.

Julian Vance stood by the floor-to-ceiling window, looking out at the rain-swept harbor. He held a crystal tumbler of amber liquid. He didn't look like a monster. He looked like a grieving politician in a bespoke suit.

He turned slowly. His face was composed, but a muscle feathered in his jaw.

"Merritt," he said, his voice smooth, cultivated. "And Mr. Ferri. You're making a terrible mess of my property."

"We're just the cleaning crew, Julian," I said.

I raised the gun.

Julian smiled, a sad, patronizing tilt of his lips. He set the drink down on his desk.

"You can't shoot me, Merritt. Think about the optics. The grieving sister-in-law murdering the city's favorite son? You'll rot in a black site."

"You think I care about optics?" I stepped closer. "I saw the cages, Julian. I saw the logs."

"Necessity," he shrugged. "Supply and demand. The world needs labor. It needs subjects. Someone has to facilitate the progress."

"Progress?" Dario's voice was low, terrifying. He holstered his gun. He walked toward the desk.

Julian's composure cracked. He took a step back.

"Stay back," Julian warned. He reached for a drawer.

I put a bullet through the wood of the desk, inches from his hand. "Don't," I said.

Dario rounded the desk. He didn't use a weapon. He used his hands.

He grabbed Julian by the lapels of his expensive Italian suit and slammed him against the blast-proof glass of the window.

"You killed my sister," Dario whispered. "You killed her husband. You tried to bury me."

"I have money!" Julian choked, his feet dangling off the floor. "I have the judges! I can give you the western territory!"

Dario looked at me over his shoulder.

"Agent Gage," he said. "Does the federal government have a use for this man?"

I looked at Julian. I saw Jack's face in the morgue. I saw the children on the boat, their eyes empty and hollowed out.

"No," I said. "Asset is burned."

Dario turned back to Julian.

"Denied," he said.

He didn't make it quick. He threw Julian to the floor.

What followed wasn't a fight. It was an execution. It was the Sword carving out the rot.

I walked to the desk. I picked up Julian's computer. I found the external drive plug. I inserted the decryption key Dario had prepped.

Downloading...

Behind me, the sounds of wet impacts and desperate, gurgling pleas filled the room. I didn't turn around. I watched the progress bar.

100%.

"Done," I said.

Silence fell behind me.

I turned.

Julian lay on the white carpet. He wasn't moving. The red stain spreading beneath him looked like a Rorschach test.

Dario stood over him, straightening his cuffs. He was breathing hard, but his face was calm. The fever in his eyes had broken.

He looked at me.

"Is it over?" he asked.

I looked at the drive in my hand. The names. The accounts. The government officials.

"The hunt is over," I said. "The war has just begun."

I walked to him. I took his bloody hand in mine. It felt right. It felt heavy.

Sirens wailed in the distance, getting louder. The police. Halloway's cleaners.

"We need to leave," I said.

Dario squeezed my hand.

"Where?"

I looked at the window, at the city sprawl that concealed a thousand other monsters.

"Anywhere we want."

I led him out of the office, stepping over the wreckage of the old world, walking into the chaos of the new one.

We were blood-soaked, exhausted, and hunted.

I had never felt more at peace.

CHAPTER TWENTY

BLOOD ON THE BALANCE SHEET

The door swung open, and the world dissolved into noise.

The warehouse floor was a twisted grid of shipping containers and shadows, a chaotic geometry designed to hide illicit cargo. Now, it was a kill box. The klaxons were deafening, a rhythmic scream that vibrated in the fillings of my teeth, but beneath that mechanical wail, I tracked the heavier thud of boots on concrete.

"Move," Dario growled.

He didn't wait for me. He surged past, moving with a predator's grace despite the bruised ribs and the tape binding his broken fingers. He raised the pistol I'd given him, cleared the corner of a crate, and fired. Two shots. Controlled. Efficient.

A guard dropped from the catwalk above, his rifle clattering against the metal railing before he hit the ground with a wet crunch.

My heart didn't hammer; it seized, holding a steady, painful rhythm against my sternum. Fear was a luxury I couldn't afford. Fear belonged to the woman who used to wear a badge and wait for backup. That woman died on the island.

We moved into the open lane.

"Contact!" a voice shouted from the gantry.

Bullets chewed up the concrete inches from my boot. Concrete dust sprayed my shins.

I didn't flinch. I raised the Glock. I didn't see a man; I saw a target acquisition profile. Center mass. The recoil jarred my wrist, a familiar, grounding shock. I hammered a volley at the suppression team on the upper rail. One man folded over the guardrail. The others ducked.

"Right flank," I shouted, my voice raw.

Dario was already there. He used a forklift as cover, firing through the gap in the protective cage. He was a creature of kinetic violence, his movements sharp and economical. Every bullet he spent purchased us another second of life.

We advanced. We weren't hiding anymore. We were cutting a path.

The air grew thick with smoke and the acrid stench of cordite. It burned my eyes, but I didn't blink. I kept my focus on the freight elevator at the far end of the facility. The only way up. The only way to Julian.

A Paladin mercenary stepped out from behind a stack of crates, leveling a submachine gun. He was ten feet away. Too close.

The barrel swung toward Dario.

"No," I hissed.

I didn't shoot. I slammed my shoulder into Dario, knocking him off balance and into the cover of a steel pillar. I took the space he had occupied. The mercenary fired.

The air snapped past my ear. Heat scorched my cheek.

I drove forward, closing the distance before he could adjust his aim. I grabbed the barrel of his weapon with my off-hand, ignoring the searing heat of the metal, and drove the ceramic knife into his throat.

He gurgled. His eyes went wide, the pupils blowing out in shock.

I ripped the blade free. He crumpled.

Dario was at my side instantly. He grabbed my arm, his grip bruising. He checked me for holes. His eyes were wild, the iris almost swallowed by the black of his pupils.

"Don't you ever," he snarled, winded and furious, "put yourself in front of a bullet for me."

"I'm the Shield," I panted, wiping blood splatter from my jaw. "Do your job. Be the Sword."

He looked at me. For a split second, the violence around us suspended. He didn't see an agent. He saw the monster he had helped create. A dark approval twisted his mouth.

"Then shield me," he said.

We moved again.

The resistance thickened near the elevator. They knew where we were going. Julian was up there, likely watching on the monitors, sipping scotch while he waited for his paid killers to wipe us off the ledger.

We took cover behind a generator. Bullets sparked off the casing.

"Cover me," Dario ordered.

He broke cover. He didn't run away from the fire; he ran perpendicular to it, drawing their eyes, drawing their aim. It was suicide. It was magnificent.

I popped up. Three guards were tracking him. Their backs were to me.

I took the shots. One. Two. Three.

Dario reached the elevator control panel. He smashed the call button with the butt of his pistol, then turned and fired blindly into the shadows to keep head down.

The heavy steel doors groaned open.

"Clear!" he shouted.

We scrambled inside. I hit the button for the Penthouse. The doors hissed shut, cutting off the deafening roar of the gunfight, sealing us in a sudden, ringing silence.

The elevator began to rise.

The box was small. Mirrors lined the walls, reflecting us back at ourselves—two blood-soaked ghosts breathing hard, smelling of sweat and murder.

I looked at him. His chest heaved. Fresh blood seeped through his shirt where the stitches on his shoulder had torn. He was barely standing, running on pure, uncut hate.

Adrenaline crashed into my system. It wasn't the flight response. It was the other thing. The life drive. The desperate need to affirm existence in the face of inevitable death.

My gaze snapped to his hands. Blood crusted the knuckles. Hands that killed. Hands that destroyed.

I needed them on me.

I slammed him against the mirrored wall. The glass groaned under the impact.

"Merritt," he growled, a warning that sounded like a plea.

I silenced him with teeth. I crushed my mouth to his, biting his lower lip until fresh blood bloomed. Iron and salt hit my tongue. Primal. There was no romance here, just the desperate hunger of two animals still breathing.

He dropped his gun. The heavy thud echoed like a gavel.

His grip bruised my hips as he hauled me up. I wrapped my legs around his waist, my thighs clamping down hard, muscles coiling tight.

"You're fucking insane," he rasped, his hand tearing at the waistband of my tactical pants.

"Fuck me," I hissed. "Right now."

He didn't hesitate. He freed himself, thick and furious. He shoved aside the fabric of my panties, his fingers grazing my clit, finding me already soaked. My body had betrayed me, slick with anticipation despite the slaughter below.

He lined up and drove home.

One thrust. He buried his cock deep inside my pussy, stretching me, filling me completely.

My head cracked back against the mirror. A gasp tore from my throat, raw and needy.

He grabbed my hair, pulling my neck back to expose the throat. "Take it," he snarled.

He pounded into me. Rough. Merciless. The friction was electric, a fire lighting up my nerve endings. He hit my cervix, that deep, aching spot that made my toes curl and my vision blur. We were ascending in a metal coffin, but I felt alive. Indestructible.

"Mine," he roared, driving harder. "You submit to this. Only this."

"Yes," I choked out. "Harder."

My pussy clamped around him, milking him, begging for his seed. I needed to feel him ruin me. The pleasure spiked, blinding and white-hot. I shrieked as I came, my body convulsing, locking him in.

He stiffened, veins bulging in his neck. He bottomed out, grinding his hips against mine.

He erupted.

Hot, thick ropes of cum shot deep inside me. He pumped into my womb, flooding me, claiming me from the inside out. He didn't pull back; he held me there, filling me until I was overflowing.

We hung there for a heartbeat, ragged and ruined, twitching in the afterglow of violence.

Then, the bell dinged.

Level P. Penthouse.

Reality slammed back into place.

Dario dropped me to my feet. He didn't say a word. He bent down, retrieved his weapon, and racked the slide. He wiped the blood from his mouth with the back of his hand.

I adjusted my clothes. I pulled the Glock from my waistband.

I looked at the reflection in the mirror one last time. My lips were swollen. My eyes were wild.

I locked the pleasure away in a steel box in the back of my mind. I would examine it later, if we survived. Right now, I needed to be sharp.

The doors opened.

The penthouse lobby was a violent contrast to the slaughter below. White marble floors. Modern art. Quiet efficiency.

Two men in suits stood by the reception desk. Paladin elite detail.

They reached for their weapons inside their jackets. Slow. So slow.

Dario took the one on the left. I took the one on the right.

Bang. Bang.

They dropped before they cleared leather.

We stepped over the bodies. The double doors to Julian's office loomed ahead. Mahogany. Heavy. Expensive.

Dario looked at me. He nodded at the door.

"Together," he said.

"Together," I answered.

He kicked the door. It flew open, slamming against the interior wall.

We walked in.

Julian Vance stood by the floor-to-ceiling window, looking out at the rain-swept harbor. He held a crystal tumbler of amber liquid. He didn't look like a monster. He looked like a grieving politician in a bespoke suit.

He turned slowly. His face was composed, but a muscle feathered in his jaw.

"Merritt," he said, his voice smooth, cultivated. "And Mr. Ferri. You're making a terrible mess of my property."

"We're just the cleaning crew, Julian," I said.

I raised the gun.

Julian smiled, a sad, patronizing tilt of his lips. He set the drink down on his desk.

"You can't shoot me, Merritt. Think about the optics. The grieving sister-in-law murdering the city's favorite son? You'll rot in a black site."

"You think I care about optics?" I stepped closer. "I saw the cages, Julian. I saw the logs."

"Necessity," he shrugged. "Supply and demand. The world needs labor. It needs subjects. Someone has to facilitate the progress."

"Progress?" Dario's voice was low, terrifying. He holstered his gun. He walked toward the desk.

Julian's composure cracked. He took a step back.

"Stay back," Julian warned. He reached for a drawer.

I put a bullet through the wood of the desk, inches from his hand. "Don't," I said.

Dario rounded the desk. He didn't use a weapon. He used his hands.

He grabbed Julian by the lapels of his expensive Italian suit and slammed him against the blast-proof glass of the window.

"You killed my sister," Dario whispered. "You killed her husband. You tried to bury me."

"I have money!" Julian choked, his feet dangling off the floor. "I have the judges! I can give you the western territory!"

Dario looked at me over his shoulder.

"Agent Gage," he said. "Does the federal government have a use for this man?"

I looked at Julian. I saw Jack's face in the morgue. I saw the children on the boat, their eyes empty and hollowed out.

"No," I said. "Asset is burned."

Dario turned back to Julian.

"Denied," he said.

He didn't make it quick. He threw Julian to the floor.

What followed wasn't a fight. It was an execution. It was the Sword carving out the rot.

I walked to the desk. I picked up Julian's computer. I found the external drive plug. I inserted the decryption key Dario had prepped.

Downloading...

Behind me, the sounds of wet impacts and desperate, gurgling pleas filled the room. I didn't turn around. I watched the progress bar.

100%.

"Done," I said.

Silence fell behind me.

I turned.

Julian lay on the white carpet. He wasn't moving. The red stain spreading beneath him looked like a Rorschach test.

Dario stood over him, straightening his cuffs. He was breathing hard, but his face was calm. The fever in his eyes had broken.

He looked at me.

"Is it over?" he asked.

I looked at the drive in my hand. The names. The accounts. The government officials.

"The hunt is over," I said. "The war has just begun."

I walked to him. I took his bloody hand in mine. It felt right. It felt heavy.

Sirens wailed in the distance, getting louder. The police. Halloway's cleaners.

"We need to leave," I said.

Dario squeezed my hand.

"Where?"

I looked at the window, at the city sprawl that concealed a thousand other monsters.

"Anywhere we want."

I led him out of the office, stepping over the wreckage of the old world, walking into the chaos of the new one.

We were blood-soaked, exhausted, and hunted.

I had never felt more at peace.

CHAPTER TWENTY-ONE

THE LAST PRAYER

The rain didn't wash the sins away. It just made the blood slicker on the concrete, turning the dock into a black mirror reflecting the ruin of the night.

I leaned against a rusted bollard, the cold metal biting into my back. My ribs were a cage of broken glass. Every breath was a negotiation with agony, a sharp, grinding reminders that I was mortal. But the pain was distant, muffled by the roar of the ocean and the singular, deafening beat of my own heart.

Merritt.

She was ten feet away, securing the mooring line of the stolen trawler. The halogen floodlight from the warehouse cut a yellow swath through the downpour, illuminating her silhouette. She moved with a jagged, desperate efficiency. She was exhausted, her movements heavy, but she didn't stop. She never stopped.

I watched her. It was a compulsion. A sickness.

The world was ending around us—sirens wailing in the distance, the smell of burning diesel choking the air—but I couldn't look anywhere else. She was the only solid thing in a universe rapidly dissolving into chaos.

She finished the knot and turned. She saw me sagging against the iron post.

She was there in a heartbeat.

"Dario." Her voice was a raw scrape of sound.

She reached for me. Her hands, cold and wet, landed on my chest. She didn't be gentle. She gripped the ruined fabric of my shirt and ripped it open, exposing the Kevlar and the skin beneath.

I hissed as the air hit the sweat-slicked bruising.

"Quiet," she ordered, her eyes dropping to my torso.

And there it was. The look.

Even here, with death closing in from the terminal gates, she looked at me with a hunger that had nothing to do with survival. Her gaze traveled over the map of violence etched into my skin—the thick cords of muscle twitching with adrenaline, the dark hair matted to my pectorals, the heavy ridge of the scar on my oblique. She didn't look away from the brutality of my body. She drank it in. Her pupils were blown wide, black holes swallowing the iris, tracking the V-taper of my hips where the gun belt hung low and heavy. She looked at me like I was a weapon she wanted to holster, a piece of art carved from granite and bad intentions. It was a possessive, terrifying scrutiny that made my blood run hot despite the freezing rain.

"You're a mess," she whispered, her thumb tracing the vein pulsing in my neck. "A beautiful, broken mess."

"I'm standing," I rasped.

"Barely." She flattened her palms against my abs, grounding herself, feeling the power I had left. "Get on the boat. I'll cast off."

"No."

I pushed off the bollard. The world tilted, then righted itself. I grabbed her wrist.

"We go together. Or we don't go."

She stared up at me, rain plastering her hair to her cheeks. She looked fierce. Lethal. The woman who had walked into hell and dragged children out by the scruff of their necks.

"Together," she agreed.

She turned toward the gangway.

A voice cut through the storm. Smooth. Cultivated. Absolute.

"Leaving so soon, Agent Gage? The service hasn't even begun."

We froze.

At the end of the pier, emerging from the shadows of a stacked container like a ghost, stood a man.

He wore a white linen suit, impeccably pressed, untouched by the filth of the terminal. He held a black umbrella in one hand and a heavy, silver-plated revolver in the other.

El Santo.

The architect. The man who whispered scripture while he broke minds.

He walked forward, his footsteps silent on the wet wood. Two massive Paladin contractors flanked him, rifles raised, faceless behind ballistic masks.

"The children," El Santo said, his voice carrying effortlessly over the wind. "They are not ready for the world. They are vessels. Unfinished."

Merritt stepped in front of me. The Shield.

"They're gone," she said, her voice steady, diamond-hard. "The van is miles away. You lose."

El Santo stopped five yards from us. He smiled. It was a gentle, pitying expression that made my skin crawl.

"Loss is a matter of perspective, my child. Suffering is the kiln. We burn the impurity to reveal the gold. Those girls... they were almost perfect. And you took them from God's light."

He raised the revolver. He didn't aim at Merritt. He aimed at me.

"Mr. Ferri," he said. "The prodigal son. You traffic in vice, yet you judge my methods. Hypocrisy is a heavy stone."

I calculated the distance. Fifteen feet. My gun was empty. I had the knife in my boot, but with two rifles trained on my center mass, I'd be dead before I cleared the leather.

I stepped sideways, trying to put myself between the muzzle and Merritt.

"Let her go," I said. My voice was low, failing. "This is business. Keep it between the men."

El Santo laughed softly. "There are no men here. Only sinners."

He cocked the hammer. *Click.*

"Kneel," he commanded. "Kneel and perhaps I will make it quick."

The contractors tightened their grip on their triggers.

I looked at Merritt. She wasn't looking at El Santo. She was looking at his hand. At the silver cross dangling from his wrist.

"I don't kneel," I snarled.

"Then you fall."

El Santo opened his mouth to speak again. To deliver the final sermon. To justify the butchery with a verse.

"The path to salvation is paved with—"

CRACK.

The sound wasn't a thunderclap. It was sharper. A flat, ugly snap.

El Santo's head snapped back. A spray of red mist erupted from his forehead, painting the inside of his pristine white umbrella.

His eyes went wide, shocked, the light extinguishing instantly.

He crumpled. The silver revolver clattered to the deck.

Merritt stood there. She held my spare SIG—the one I kept in the ankle rig she must have swiped when she checked my legs. She hadn't hesitated. She hadn't warned him. She hadn't let him finish his sentence.

The two contractors froze. For a split second, the chain of command shattered. Their principal was dead.

That second was enough.

I moved.

Pain vanished. The only thing that existed was the kill.

I lunged at the guard on the right. I drove my shoulder into his chest, knocking him off the pier. He splashed into the black water below, his rifle firing uselessly into the air.

Merritt pivoted. She fired two rounds into the chest of the second guard.

Thud. Thud.

The armor held, but the impact staggered him.

I didn't wait. I grabbed the fallen revolver—El Santo's gun—from the wet wood. I came up in a crouch.

I put a bullet through the guard's visor.

He dropped like a stone.

Silence slammed back down on the dock, heavier than before.

El Santo lay in a heap of white linen and blood. The rain was already diluting the red pool spreading around his head.

Merritt lowered the gun. She stared at the body. Her chest heaved.

"He talks too much," she said.

I looked at her.

She was terrifying. She was the most magnificent thing God ever made.

"Merritt," I breathed.

She turned to me. The adrenaline was crashing now. Her hands started to shake.

"Get on the boat," she said, her voice trembling. "Dario, move."

We scrambled up the gangway. I untied the stern line. She hit the ignition.

The twin diesels roared to life, a guttural growl that vibrated through the hull.

I limped to the cockpit. Merritt throttled up. The boat surged forward, the bow cutting through the chop, putting distance between us and the carnage.

We didn't look back at the terminal. We didn't look back at the bodies or the life we were leaving behind.

We hit the open water. The ocean was a vast, indifferent void.

Merritt killed the throttle once we were three miles out. She set the autopilot to a heading that pointed nowhere. Just West. Just away.

The silence in the cabin was thick.

She stepped away from the console. She turned to me.

Useable light from the instrument panel washed over us in greens and reds.

"Is it done?" she asked. A whisper.

I looked at her hands. They were stained with gun oil and blood.

"The head is cut," I said. "The body will thrash for a while. But it's dead."

She nodded. Then, the strength finally left her.

She stumbled.

I caught her.

I pulled her into me, ignoring the scream of my ribs. I buried my face in her neck, inhaling the scent of rain, copper, and her.

"You saved me," I murmured against her skin.

"I claimed you," she corrected, her fingers digging into my back. "There's a difference."

I pulled back to look at her. Her eyes were dark, exhausted, but clear. There was no regret in them. The broken shield had forged itself into a sword.

"Where do we go?" I asked.

She reached up. She touched the bruise on my cheekbone. Her thumb brushed my lip.

"It doesn't matter," she said. "As long as they can't find us."

I leaned into her touch. The obsession uncoiled in my chest, settling into a permanent, heavy weight. I belonged to this. I belonged to her.

"They won't find us," I promised. "I'll burn the map."

She rested her forehead against mine.

"Good."

Outside, the storm raged on, thrashing the ocean into whitecaps. But inside the cabin, in the small space between our bodies, everything was quiet.

We were murderers. We were saviors.

We were free.

CHAPTER TWENTY-TWO

SOVEREIGN TERRITORY

The ocean wasn't blue. It was a flat, heaving slab of obsidian that swallowed the world whole.

I gripped the wheel of the trawler, my knuckles bleached white against the rusted metal. The diesel engine thundered beneath the deck plates, a rhythmic, mechanical heartbeat that vibrated straight up through the soles of my boots and settled in my teeth.

We were three miles out. Maybe four. The coast was a smear of light pollution on the horizon, a glowing bruise where the city bled into the sky.

I didn't look at it.

My chest ached. Not a sharp pain, but a hollow, scraping sensation, as if someone had scooped out the lungs and the heart and the conscience and replaced them with wet sand. I breathed in salt spray and diesel fumes. It tasted like freedom. It tasted like ash.

"Merritt."

The name was a rasp, barely audible over the engine's roar.

I locked the wheel. The autopilot engaged with a sullen click, holding the heading: West. Just West. Away from the flashing lights, the crime scene tape, and the hollow eulogies they would read for us on the morning news.

I turned.

Dario sat on the metal bench against the starboard bulkhead. He looked like a ruin. His bespoke suit was gone, shredded and discarded on the dock. He wore a tactical undershirt that was more hole than fabric, slick with seawater and the dark, glossy sheen of arterial blood.

He wasn't looking at the horizon. He was watching me.

His eyes were dilated, the black pupils swallowing the iris, burning with a fever that had nothing to do with infection. He looked at me like I was the only solid thing in a universe that had disintegrated.

I walked to him. The deck pitched. I moved with it.

I dropped to my knees between his legs.

The position was familiar. Submissive. Vulnerable. But the air between us had shifted. I wasn't kneeling to beg. I was kneeling to salvage.

I reached for the hem of his ruined shirt. My hands were filthy—grease, gun oil, and the dried blood of the man I had executed on the pier.

"This is going to hurt," I said. My voice sounded strange. Flat. The voice of a woman who had forgotten how to apologize.

"Good," he ground out.

I peeled the fabric away from his ribs. The Kevlar vest had stopped the bullets, but the kinetic energy had done its work. His torso was a canvas of violence—deep purple bruising, lacerations from the shrapnel, the angry red weeping of the graze on his oblique.

I poured the antiseptic.

He didn't flinch. His muscles jumped, hard cords of tension snapping beneath the skin, but he didn't pull away. He leaned into it. He leaned into me.

I pressed a sterile pad against the worst of it. The white gauze turned red instantly.

The heat of him radiated against my face. It was suffocating. Intoxicating.

I looked at my hands. They were covered in his blood.

Ten hours ago, I was a Special Agent. I was the line in the sand. I wore a badge that said I protected the innocent and upheld the law.

Now, I was kneeling in the belly of a stolen boat, my hands painted in the blood of a mob boss, and I didn't want to wash it off.

The realization hit me with the force of a rogue wave. It wasn't disgust. It was baptism.

I wasn't the Shield anymore. A shield deflects. A shield takes the blow and stays clean on the other side.

I was the sponge. I had soaked it all up—the violence, the hate, the absolute necessity of the kill.

"You're thinking too loud," Dario whispered. His hand moved, heavy and uncoordinated, landing on the back of my neck. His thumb pressed into the base of my skull.

"I killed him," I said. I looked up. "El Santo. I didn't arrest him. I didn't read him his rights. I just... ended him."

Dario's grip tightened. Grounding me. "He needed ending."

"I enjoyed it."

The confession hung in the salty air.

Dario leaned forward. His forehead rested against mine. He smelled of rain and iron.

"The law is a fairy tale we tell people so they can sleep at night," he murmured. "But we woke up, Merritt. We woke up in the dark."

I closed my eyes. I could still feel the recoil of the revolver in my hand. The snap of the trigger. The permanence of it.

"I'm a monster," I breathed.

"No." His lips brushed mine. A grazing contact that sent a jolt of electricity straight to my groin. "You're free. Monsters don't have to look in the mirror and pretend they see a saint. They just feed."

I opened my eyes. I looked at him. Really looked at him.

He was broken. He was lethal. And he was mine.

I pressed my hand flat against the center of his chest, over the slow, thudding drum of his heart. I smeared the blood there, marking him.

"Then we feed," I whispered.

The radio on the console crackled to life, shattering the moment.

"...Coast Guard Sector San Diego, be advised. Suspect vessel is a forty-foot trawler, heading two-seven-zero. Fugitives are considered armed and extremely dangerous. Federal warrants issued for Agent Merritt Gage and Dario Ferri. Approach with caution..."

The voice of the System. The voice of the Director. The voice of the world that wanted to put us in a cage, categorize us, label us, and bury us under a mountain of redacted paperwork.

They wanted to make us a tragedy. A rogue agent and a criminal, gone mad with grief.

I stood up. My knees cracked on the hard deck.

I walked to the console.

The radio kept spitting static and codes. Numbers that defined our lives. Coordinates that tried to pin us to a map.

I gripped the cord of the handset.

I didn't turn the volume down. I ripped the entire unit out of the housing.

Wires sparked. Plastic snapped. The voice died mid-sentence.

I walked to the open door of the cabin and threw the radio into the ocean.

Splash. Silence. The black water swallowed it whole.

I turned back to Dario.

He watched me from the shadows of the bench. A dark approval twisted his mouth.

"No map," he said.

"No map," I agreed.

I walked back to him. I didn't check the course. I didn't check the fuel. We had enough to get to Mexican waters. To the ghost towns where money bought silence and violence bought respect.

I sat next to him on the bench. The space was cramped. Our thighs touched. The contact was solid, heavy, real.

He reached into his pocket and pulled out something small. It glinted in the dim red light of the instrument panel.

A zip tie. Black, heavy-duty plastic. The kind we used on the raid. The kind used to bind wrists.

He held it up.

"I don't have a ring," he said. His voice was rough, stripping the gears. "And I don't have a priest."

I looked at the plastic loop. It was ugly. Utilitarian. It was exactly right.

"I don't believe in God anymore," I said. "So a priest would be a waste of time."

He took my left wrist. His touch was possessive, bruising. He slid the plastic band over my wrist, cinching it tight—not enough to cut circulation, but enough to be felt. Enough to be a constant, biting reminder of who held the leash.

"Sovereign territory," he growled. "You belong to the war. You belong to me."

I looked at the black band against my pale skin. It looked better than gold. It looked like survival.

"And you," I said, leaning in until our mouths were inches apart. "You belong to the woman who pulled you out of the fire."

He didn't smile. He didn't have to.

"Until the fire burns out," he promised.

I kissed him. It tasted of salt and blood and a future that was terrifyingly blank.

Outside, the ocean stretched on forever, a vast, indifferent void waiting to be filled. We drifted into the dark, two predators finally off the chain, leaving the lights of the civilized world behind us to drown.

CHAPTER TWENTY-THREE

CHAMPAGNE AND GUN OIL

S ix Months Later.

The ocean view from the terrace of the Malibu estate didn't look like a painting. It looked like a border. A restless, liquid line separating the civilized world from the chaos we swam in.

Merritt stood at the glass railing. The wind off the Pacific whipped the silk of her robe against her legs, but she didn't move. She never flinched at the elements anymore. She absorbed them.

I sat in the high-backed leather chair inside the master suite, cleaning the disassembled slide of my custom Beretta. The smell of Hoppe's No. 9 solvent filled the air, sharp and chemical, mixing with the scent of the expensive espresso on the table. It was the perfume of our new life. Luxury and lethality, shaken together and served over ice.

The silence in the room wasn't empty. It was pressurized.

Six months ago, we were bleeding out on a stolen trawler, running from every badge in the hemisphere. Now, we owned the coast. Not legally—the law was still a clumsy instrument we had learned to bypass—but practically. We were the ghosts the cartels whispered about. The monsters the traffickers checked under their beds for.

Merritt turned. The sun caught the angles of her face, highlighting the faint scar on her cheekbone where the debris from the explosion had grazed her. She didn't cover it with makeup. She wore it like a medal.

"The shipment docked," she said. Her voice was low, devoid of the frantic energy that used to drive her. Now, she spoke with the terrifying calm of a woman who held the detonator.

I wiped the firing pin with a rag. "Any issues?"

"The port authority asked questions. I sent them the photos of the Director leaving the brothel in Tijuana. The questions stopped."

I reassembled the pistol. *Click. Snap.* The sound was satisfyingly final.

"Leverage," I said, setting the gun down next to the coffee cup. "It travels faster than a bullet."

She walked into the room. Her bare feet made no sound on the polished concrete floor. She moved like smoke, like something that could slip through a crack in the wall and kill you before you woke up.

"It's not just leverage, Dario. It's the truth. We just happen to be the only ones willing to weaponize it."

She stopped in front of me. She looked at the gun, then at my hands. Her eyes were dark, dilated pools of intelligence and trauma.

"You're restless," she observed.

"I'm awake."

"Same thing."

She reached out and traced the line of the tattoo on my forearm—the coordinate of the island where we burned the world down. Her fingers were cool.

"The Senate committee ruled the explosion an accident," she said, reciting the headline we had bought and paid for. "A gas leak in the facility's generator room. No survivors. Case closed."

"And us?"

"Retired. Deceased. Disappeared. Pick your favorite lie."

I grabbed her wrist. I didn't pull. I just held her there, feeling the steady drum of her pulse against my thumb.

"I prefer 'Reborn'."

She looked down at me. A small, dangerous smile touched her lips.

"That sounds religious. I thought we killed God on the pier."

"We replaced him."

She stepped between my legs. The silk robe fell open, revealing the pale skin of her thighs, the curve of her hip. I rested my hands on her waist, grounding myself. The heat of her body was the only thing that kept the coldness in my chest from spreading.

We were damaged goods. Both of us. The violence hadn't left us; it had just settled into the foundation, hardening the concrete. We slept with weapons on the nightstands. We scanned exits when we entered restaurants. We didn't trust the peace. We just managed the war.

"Turn around," I said.

The command was soft, but the weight behind it was granite.

She didn't hesitate. She turned her back to me, dropping to her knees on the rug between my boots. She swept her hair off her neck, exposing the nape.

The submission wasn't about powerlessness. It was about trust. It was the Shield lowering its guard because it knew the Sword was behind it.

I reached into the pocket of my slacks.

The collar was leather. Black. Thin. Lined with soft suede but reinforced with a steel core. It had a small silver ring at the front. No name tag. No jewels. Just function.

I draped it around her throat.

For a second, I paused. I felt the tension in her shoulders, the way she braced herself. Not against pain, but against the memory of the chaos. The noise of the world outside—the politics, the lies, the buzzing of the phones—it all tried to pull her apart. It tried to make her Merritt Gage, the disgraced agent. The rogue. The victim.

This strip of leather stopped the noise. It created a boundary. Inside the circle, she wasn't a statistic. She was mine. And because she was mine, nothing could hurt her without going through me first.

I fastened the buckle. *Snick.*

She exhaled. A long, shuddering release of air. Her shoulders dropped two inches.

I ran my thumb over the leather.

"You're safe," I murmured against the back of her ear. "You're grounded."

"I know," she whispered. She leaned back against my legs, closing her eyes. "It's the only time the screaming stops."

"Let them scream. We aren't listening."

I kept my hand on her neck, feeling the vibration of her voice, the beat of her life. This was the ritual. The recalibration. Every morning, we reminded ourselves of the hierarchy. Not Master and Slave in the way the books wrote it. But Anchor and Ship.

She needed the weight to keep from drifting. I needed the ship to have a reason to hold the line.

"The Director called the secure line again," she said, her eyes still closed. "He wants to know if we're willing to consult on the border crisis."

"Tell him to go to hell."

"I told him our fee doubled."

I laughed. It was a low, rusty sound. "Mercenary."

"Pragmatist. If they want us to clean up their messes, they pay for the bleach."

She opened her eyes and looked at the reflection in the glass door. She touched the collar. The look on her face wasn't shame. It was relief.

"We have a problem," she said, the tone shifting instantly. The vulnerability vanished, replaced by the steel of the operative.

"What kind?"

"The kind that bleeds."

She stood up. The movement was fluid. She walked to the desk in the corner and tapped the keyboard. The massive monitor on the wall flickered to life.

Satellite imagery. Grainy black and white thermal feeds.

"Baja coast," she said, pointing to a cluster of heat signatures on a remote beach. "Thirty miles south of our old playground."

I stood and walked to the screen. I recognized the terrain. Smuggler's coves. Places where the tide washed away the evidence.

"Who?" I asked.

"Not Cartel. The movement patterns are wrong. Too disciplined for sicarios. Too sloppy for Feds."

She tapped a key. The image zoomed in.

Detailed shots of men unloading crates from a Zodiac. They weren't moving bricks of cocaine. They were moving heavy cases. Long. Rectangular.

"Weapons," I noted.

"MANPADS," she corrected. "Shoulder-fired anti-air missiles. Russian make, likely SA-24s."

She pulled up a dossier. Faces. grainy surveillance photos taken from a drone.

"Intel suggests a splinter cell. Somali nationals leveraging the refugee routes, funded by money moving through Dubai. They aren't looking to cross the border to work. They're looking to set up a firing solution on the flight path into LAX."

I stared at the screen. The audacity of it. In my backyard.

The Cartel was a business. They sold vice. I understood them. I could negotiate with them. But this? This was ideology. This was chaos for the sake of chaos.

"They're on my coast," I said. The temperature in the room dropped ten degrees.

"They paid off the Sinaloa lieutenants to look the other way," Merritt said. "But they didn't pay us."

She looked at me. The collar around her neck stood out against her pale skin, a black line of separation. Above it, her face was a mask of cold fury.

"The Agency can't touch them down there," she said. "Jurisdiction issues. Diplomatic red tape. By the time they get a Predator drone authorized, those missiles will be in a van heading north."

"We don't have jurisdiction issues," I said.

"No. We have a boat."

I looked at the Beretta on the table. Then I looked at the woman who had burned a trafficking ring to the ground because she found a dog she liked.

"How many?" I asked.

"Twelve hostiles. Heavy weapons."

"Light work."

I walked to the walk-in closet. It wasn't filled with suits anymore. One side was lined with bespoke Italian wool. The other side was a wall of tactical gear.

I pulled out a plate carrier. Matte black. No patches. No flags.

I tossed Merritt hers. She caught it one-handed.

"Load up," I ordered. "We leave in twenty."

She dropped the silk robe. She didn't look at me for approval. She dressed with the efficiency of a soldier. Compression gear. Cargo pants. Boots. The transition from lover to killer was instant, terrifying, and seamless.

She strapped the plate carrier over her chest. She checked the ceramic plates.

Then she walked to the gun safe.

She pulled out a suppressed MP5. She racked the slide, checking the chamber.

"Do we take prisoners?" she asked.

I pulled a combat knife from the rack and sheathed it on my belt. The steel felt familiar. Right.

"Prisoners require paperwork," I said. "And I'm retired."

She grinned. It was a sharp, wolfish expression.

"Scrub the site," she said.

"Burn it all."

We walked out of the bedroom.

Downstairs, the house was quiet. The expansive living room, with its white furniture and art deco statues, felt like a museum exhibit we were just visiting.

We reached the garage.

The Aston Martin was parked next to a black armored SUV.

We took the truck.

I threw the gear bags in the back. Merritt climbed into the passenger seat. She had a laptop open on her knees, already hacking the local harbor comms to clear our exit.

I got in behind the wheel. The engine roared to life—eight cylinders of American anger.

I looked at her.

The sunlight hit the silver ring on her collar.

"You good?" I asked.

She looked up from the screen. Her eyes were clear. The shadows were gone, burned away by the focus on the mission.

"I'm exactly where I'm supposed to be," she said.

"And where is that?"

"Hunting with the devil."

I put the truck in gear. The garage door opened, revealing the blinding white light of the California afternoon.

"Let's go do God's work," I said.

"God is busy," Merritt replied, chambering a round. "We'll handle it."

We rolled out of the compound, the tires crunching on the gravel. We didn't look back at the luxury, the peace, or the safety we had built.

Those things were for the people we protected.

For us, there was only the hunt.

The road wound down the cliffs toward the water. We descended into the smog and the heat, two shadows moving against the glare.

The world thought we were villains. The government thought we were liabilities. The history books would forget us entirely.

That was fine.

Legends didn't need to be written down. They just needed to be feared.

I accelerated. Merritt checked her ammo count.

We drove into the sun, ready to make the darkness bleed.

[THE END]

CHAPTER TWENTY-FOUR

SOVEREIGN TERRITORY

T he engine of the armored truck ticked as it cooled, the metal contracting in the silence of the garage. The sound was a rhythmic, dying heartbeat in the cavernous space.

I didn't move to open the door. I just sat there, gripping the wheel, the leather warm and damp against my palms. Beside me, Merritt exhaled—a long, shuddering release that fogged the passenger window.

We smelled of cordite, salt, and the metallic tang of other men's blood. It was a perfume that should have been repulsive in the sanctuary of this estate. Instead, it felt like the only honest scent in California.

"Twelve," she said, her voice rough, stripped of the polish she used for the politicians. "We got all twelve."

"We cleared the board," I corrected. "They were just pieces."

I turned to look at her.

The adrenaline was fading, leaving behind that dangerous, hollow clarity that comes after the kill. She was staring at her hands, turning them over as if checking for stains that wouldn't wash off.

I watched her, and the obsession I usually kept leashed in the back of my mind lunged forward, snapping its teeth.

It wasn't just admiration for her efficiency. Any soldier could double-tap a target. It was the way her soul seemed to vibrate at the exact same frequency as mine. I looked at the dark smudges of grease on her cheek, the feral brightness in her eyes that the fatigue couldn't dim, and I felt a hunger so sharp it felt like a knife in the gut. I didn't just want her here; I wanted to crack her open and crawl inside the wreckage of her history, to nest in the broken places where the world had failed her. She was a mirror, reflecting back every jagged, ugly thing I was, and God help me, I wanted to smash the glass just to see if we bled the same color.

"Dario," she said. She didn't look up, but her hand moved, covering mine on the gear shift. Her fingers were cold. "Take me inside. Before the ghosts catch up."

I opened the door.

We walked into the house. It wasn't a home. It was a monument to isolation, a sprawling expanse of glass and Italian marble designed to keep the world at arm's length.

We tracked sand and oil across the pristine white floor of the foyer. I didn't care. Let the maid clean it. Let the evidence of what we were stain the perfection.

We didn't speak. We moved with the synchronized gravity of binary stars, orbiting a shared center of gravity that pulled us toward the master suite.

I kicked the door shut behind us.

"Strip," I ordered.

Merritt was already unclipping the plate carrier. It hit the floor with a heavy thud. Then the combat shirt. The cargo pants. The boots.

She stood in the center of the room, naked, her skin pale and luminous against the dark shadows of the coastline outside. Bruises were already blooming on her shoulder where the rifle stock had kicked.

She looked at me. Waiting.

I pulled off my own gear. The vest. The holster. The blood-stiffened shirt.

I stood before her, the magical hum of my Shield finally dying out, leaving nothing between us but air and intent.

Her eyes drifted over me, heavy with a hunger that bordered on starvation. She didn't look at me with tenderness; she looked at me with a desperate, dehydrating thirst. Her pupils dilated, swallowing the iris as she tracked the thick slabs of muscle across my chest, the roped veins traversing my biceps, the violent topography of raised white scars mapping my torso. Her gaze fell to my hands—hands that had just snapped a man's neck an hour ago—and her breath hitched, a wet, needy sound. She looked at me like I was a loaded weapon she wanted to pull the trigger on, desperate to feel the recoil shudder through her own flesh.

"You're terrifying," she whispered, stepping into my reach. Her fingers grazed the hair on my chest, trembling. "You look like something carved out of granite and bad intentions. God, I want you to wreck me."

"Careful, Merritt," I rasped, snagging her wrist. My voice was a low grind of gravel. "I might not stop."

"Don't."

I swept her up. Her legs locked around my waist, face burying in the crook of my neck, inhaling the scent of violence and sweat.

We didn't trip toward the bed. I carried her into the shower.

I kicked the glass door shut and wrenched the handle. The water hit us freezing cold, a biting shock against the fever heat rolling off our skin.

She gasped, arching into the spray. The water swirling at the drain turned a pale, diluted pink—sand, sweat, and dried blood washing away.

I slammed her back against the freezing mosaic. My hands bruised her hips, fingers digging into the soft, yielding flesh that begged to be marked.

"Take it," I growled.

"Everything," she panted, wrapping her legs around my waist. "Break me."

I drove my cock deep inside her. Her pussy was tight, a wet, suffocating vice that clamped down on me with greedy desperation. She screamed, a raw, glorious sound torn from her throat as I stretched her limits, punishing her with pleasure. Merritt didn't shrink away; she arched into the invasion, her nails raking down my spine to open fresh wounds.

We fucked with the frantic rhythm of survival. The smack of wet skin echoed like gunshots. Water cascaded over us, cold biting against the friction burn, but we only felt the heat. She convulsed around me, her inner walls milking me, forcing my release. I groaned, losing control, pumping hot strands of cum deep into her womb, claiming her completely. I kept thrusting until I was empty, letting her overflow, my seed mixing with the diluted blood swirling at our feet.

She slumped against me, eyes glazed and wrecked. Beautiful. The adrenaline crash finally hit, leaving us heavy, anchored to the earth by the weight of what we'd just done.

*

Twenty minutes later, we were on the terrace.

The sun was dipping below the horizon, bleeding orange and violet into the Pacific. The air had cooled, but the heat between us remained, a banked fire.

Merritt wore one of my white dress shirts, the cuffs rolled up to her elbows. She leaned against the railing, her hair damp and slicked back, holding a glass of bourbon I had poured her.

I stood behind her. I wasn't drinking. I was watching the perimeter, a habit I would never break.

"The news cycle is already spinning," she said, looking out at the water. "Reports of a gas main explosion in a warehouse near Ensenada. No survivors. Local authorities are investigating."

"Let them investigate ash," I said.

"The Director knows."

"The Director suspects," I corrected. "There's a difference. Suspicion is a ghost. Evidence is a body. We gave them neither."

She turned to face me. The wind whipped the oversized shirt around her legs. She looked small in it, but I knew better. I knew the steel that ran down her spine.

"I took it off," she said softly.

I looked at her naked throat.

"I know."

She reached into the pocket of the shirt and pulled out the black leather collar. The silver ring caught the dying light.

"It's a liability in the field," she said. "Snag hazard. Identification marker."

"Valid."

"But I'm not in the field anymore."

She held it out to me. Her hand was steady. Her eyes were clear, ancient, and absolutely certain.

I took the leather strip. It was warm from her body heat.

"You understand what this means, Merritt?" I asked, my voice low. "This isn't jewelry. It's a heavy thing to wear. It means you don't get to run when the darkness gets too loud. It means you stay here, in the fire, with me."

"I told you," she said, lifting her chin, exposing the vulnerable column of her neck. "I don't want to run. I want to burn."

I stepped into her space. I felt the magnetic pull of her submission, the way she softened only for me, the way the Shield lowered its guard because it knew the Sword was standing watch.

I draped the leather around her throat.

For a second, my knuckles brushed her pulse point. It was hammering. A frantic, bird-like rhythm against the calm surface of her resolve.

I fastened the buckle. *Snick.*

The sound was a lock turning. A finality.

She let out a breath, her shoulders dropping, the tension draining out of her frame as if the collar were a physical weight grounding her to the floor.

She reached up and touched the silver ring.

"Better," she whispered.

"You belong to the war," I said, repeating the vow we made in the dark.

"And to you," she finished.

She leaned her forehead against my chest. I wrapped my arms around her, pulling her in, burying my face in her damp hair. We stood there as the sun vanished and the world turned gray.

We were monsters. We were murderers. We had more blood on our hands than most dictators.

But standing there, holding the woman who had walked into hell and pulled me out by the scruff of my neck, I didn't feel like a villain.

I felt like a king in a fortress that no army could breach.

"What now?" she mumbled against my shirt.

I looked out at the ocean. The waves were black now, rolling in from the dark, endless and indifferent.

"Now," I said, tightening my grip on her. "We wait for them to make a mistake."

"And when they do?"

I smiled. It was a cold, brutal expression that no one but her would ever see.

"Then we remind them why they should have stayed afraid of the dark."

Merritt lifted her head. She traced the line of my jaw with her thumb.

"I love it when you talk like a psychopath," she murmured.

"I love it when you listen."

She laughed—a true, unburdened sound that was the rarest thing in my life.

We turned back to the view. The lights of the coast were flickering on, a string of pearls along the throat of the beast.

Let the world spin. Let the agencies file their reports and the politicians make their speeches.

We were here. We were armed. And we were finally, undeniably free.

[THE END]

CHAPTER TWENTY-FIVE

EMPIRE OF INK AND LEAD

The glass walls of our new office didn't offer a view. They offered a target list.

San Diego sprawled beneath us, a grid of corruption and commerce bleeding into the black Pacific. From up here, the people looked like ants, and the cars looked like blood cells moving through a concrete artery. I stood at the window, my reflection ghosting over the city lights. The woman in the glass wore black silk and diamonds, but her eyes belonged to a wolf that had chewed its foot off to escape a trap.

Behind me, the air in the room felt heavy, displaced by the sheer mass of the man sitting on the corner of the mahogany desk.

Dario cleaned his nails with a stiletto. The rhythmic *snick* of steel against keratin was the only sound in the room.

Across from us, Director Halloway sweated through his cheap government suit. He sat on the edge of the low leather chair, clutching a briefcase that contained threats he no longer had the teeth to enforce.

"We need a decision, Agent Gage," Halloway said. His voice cracked. He tried to cover it with a cough, but the weakness hung in the recycled air. "The Bureau is willing to overlook the... irregularities... in Baja. But we need the drives. The intel you pulled from the island."

I didn't turn around. I watched a police cruiser flash its lights on the highway below.

"Irregularities," I repeated. The word tasted like copper.

"You burned a sovereign facility to the ground," Halloway snapped, finding a scrap of courage. "You executed a foreign national. You stole millions in unmarked cryptocurrency. That's not field work, Merritt. That's domestic terrorism."

"It was justice," Dario said. He didn't look up from the knife. "Your version of justice requires paperwork. Ours requires gasoline."

Halloway shifted his gaze to Dario, then quickly back to the floor. "Mr. Ferri. Your involvement complicates things. But the offer stands. Full immunity. Reinstatement. All we need is the location of the surviving children and the encryption keys."

I turned.

The movement silenced him.

I walked to the table. My heels clicked on the marble floor—sharp, deliberate strikes. I didn't sit. I stood over him. The Shield was gone. The Sword was in my hand, forged from ones and zeros.

"You think this is a negotiation," I said softly.

"It is," Halloway insisted, though his eyes darted to the door. "We can freeze your assets. We can put your faces on every screen in America."

I picked up the tablet from the table and slid it across to him.

"Open it."

Halloway hesitated. Then his trembling fingers tapped the screen.

His face went gray. All the blood drained out of him, leaving him looking like wet newsprint.

"This..." He swallowed hard. "Where did you get this?"

"The dark web has a memory," I said. "And so do I. That's you, Director. Six months ago. Tijuana. The 'gentlemen's club' run by the cartel lieutenant we just put in the ground. The timestamps match your 'diplomatic summit' in Mexico City."

Halloway closed the tablet. He looked sick.

"What do you want?"

"I want you to leave," I said. "And I want you to tell your superiors that Merritt Gage is dead. She died on that island. The woman running this city is someone else entirely."

"They won't stop," Halloway whispered. "The machine never stops."

"Then we break the gears."

Dario stood up. He moved with the sudden, terrifying grace of a landslide. He walked to Halloway, plucked the briefcase from his hands, and tossed it into the trash can.

"Get out," Dario rumbled.

Halloway scrambled up. He didn't look back. He ran.

The heavy door clicked shut, sealing us in the silence.

I stared at the wood grain. My heart hammered against my ribs—not from fear, but from the adrenaline of the kill. It was a different kind of violence. Clean. Cold. Bloodless.

"He'll retire within the week," Dario said. He walked up behind me.

I didn't need to turn to know he was there. The temperature in the room shifted. The air charged with static.

"He has no choice," I replied. "I own his pension. I own his reputation. I own the ink on his obituary."

Dario's hands settled on my waist. Heavy. Possessive. His thumbs pressed into the soft flesh above my hips, grounding me before I could float away into the ether of my own head.

"You're shaking," he murmured against my ear.

"It's the crash."

"No." He turned me around. "It's the hunger."

He looked down at me. The scar above his eye was white against his tanned skin. His eyes were black pits of absolute focus. He saw everything—the cracks in the armor, the fatigue eating at my marrow, the desperate need to be held down so I didn't shatter.

"Tell me who you are," he ordered. The command wasn't a question. It was a calibration.

I reached up. My fingers brushed the collar hidden beneath the high neck of my silk blouse. The leather was warm, a secret weight against my throat.

"I'm the one who burns the map," I whispered.

"And?"

"I'm yours."

He didn't kiss me. He claimed me.

His mouth crushed down on mine, devouring the protest, the logic, the lingering noise of the outside world. It tasted of expensive scotch and violence. He lifted me, setting me on the edge of the desk, sweeping the tablet and the crystal decanter onto the floor.

Glass shattered. Neither of us flinched.

His hands were everywhere—rough, demanding, tearing at the silk. He needed flesh. He needed to verify that we were still solid, still here, still breathing after wading through so much death.

I wrapped my legs around him, pulling him closer, desperate for the friction. My nails dug into the muscles of his back, scraping over the scars I had memorized in the dark.

"Make it quiet," I begged against his lips. "Dario, please. Make it stop."

"I've got you," he growled. "I'm the wall. Slam against me."

He drove into me, a hard, rhythmic collision that jarred the breath from my lungs. It wasn't gentle. We didn't do gentle. Gentle was a lie told by people who hadn't seen the world with its skin peeled back. This was survival. This was two broken things fusing together under extreme heat and pressure.

Every thrust chipped away at the polished exterior I wore for the public. The media mogul vanished. The federal agent vanished. There was only the woman, raw and open, anchored to the earth by the man who held her throat.

"Mine," he snarled, his hand tightening on my hip, leaving a bruise that would bloom like a dark flower by morning. "Sovereign territory. No one touches this. No one touches you."

"Only you," I gasped, head thrown back, staring at the ceiling as the pleasure spiked, sharp and blinding. "Only you."

The release hit us both like a physical blow. We broke apart and came back together, shuddering, sweating, breathing the same air in the wreckage of the office.

Silence returned, but it wasn't heavy anymore. It was settled.

Dario rested his forehead against mine. His heart thundered against my chest, a war drum beating a retreat.

We stayed like that for a long time, surrounded by broken glass and the ruins of a government career, absolute rulers of a kingdom built on secrets.

*

Six Months Later

The dawn was gray and cold, a marine layer hugging the coastline like a wet shroud.

I stood on the tarmac of the private airstrip, the wind whipping strands of hair across my face. The Gulfstream jet idled nearby, its engines whining in a high-pitched scream.

Dario slammed the trunk of the black SUV. He walked toward me, carrying two heavy duffel bags. He wore casual tactical gear—coyote brown pants, a black fitted shirt, and boots that had seen more war zones than most infantry battalions.

He dropped the bags at my feet.

"Loadout is checked," he said. "Suppressors, thermal optics, and the rebreathers."

I checked my watch. "The pilot says we have a four-hour window before the storm hits the Horn of Africa."

"Plenty of time."

He looked at me. I wasn't wearing silk today. I was wearing the gear. The ceramic plates in my carrier pressed familiarly against my ribs. The weight of the Sig Sauer on my thigh was a comfort, not a burden.

We weren't running. We weren't hiding.

The intelligence had come in two days ago. A new cell. ISIS operatives moving under the guise of Somali refugees, trying to establish a foothold on the shipping lanes. They thought the ocean was big enough to hide them.

They were wrong.

The world thought we were retired. The media ran stories about my philanthropy. The government had redacted our files until we were ghosts.

But ghosts still haunt.

"You ready?" Dario asked. He reached out and adjusted the strap of my rifle bag. His knuckles grazed my cheek—a tender touch from a hand that could kill in a second.

I looked at the jet. Then I looked at him.

Six months of peace. Six months of sleeping in the same bed, of waking up without screaming, of coffee on the terrace and dinners in the city. We had built a life. A good one.

But the itch was always there. The knowledge that out there, in the dark, things were crawling that needed to be stepped on.

"I tried knitting," I said, a dry smile touching my lips. "I wasn't very good at it."

Dario grinned. It was the wolf's grin, sharp and full of teeth.

"You kept stabbing the yarn."

"It looked suspicious."

He laughed, a low rumble that vibrated in my chest. He grabbed the back of my neck, pulling me in for a kiss that tasted of coffee and anticipation.

"Let's go to work," he said against my mouth.

"Do we have a return flight booked?"

"Open ended," he replied, pulling back to look into my eyes. "We come back when the list is empty."

"The list is never empty, Dario."

"Then we never stop."

He picked up the bags. I grabbed the hard case containing the drone tech.

We walked toward the stairs of the jet.

The wind picked up, howling across the tarmac, trying to push us back. We leaned into it. We walked side by side, our strides matching, two apex predators returning to the wild.

The world was full of monsters.

But we were the ones they checked the closet for.

We boarded the plane. The door sealed shut with a hiss of pressurized air.

We were gone.